THE ANGEL ISLAND

DARK WORLD: THE ANGEL TRIALS 5

MICHELLE MADOW

DREAMSCAPE PUBLISHING

RAVEN

*W*itches dressed in matching white outfits teleported into the bunker to bring all of us to the Haven. I wasn't sure why they were all dressed the same, but they looked like they'd come straight from a yoga retreat.

There were thirty-nine of us that needed transportation. Thirty-six gifted humans (I was one of them), one vampire (Thomas), one shifter (Noah), and one male witch (Dr. Foster.)

Oh, and one dead witch. Cassandra.

So, forty of us needed transportation.

I couldn't look at where Cassandra was lying in a puddle of her own blood. Thomas was huddled by her side, devastated. He wasn't looking at anything but her.

From the little I knew, the two of them had been like family. My heart broke for him.

I hadn't let go of Noah's hand since he'd rushed into the bunker, killed the demon guards, and saved the day.

Now a kind looking witch approached me and held her hand out for me to take. "Ready?" she asked.

I glanced over to Noah, my heart racing at the thought of leaving him so soon. We'd only just been reunited. I knew we had to all get to the Haven, but couldn't Noah and I teleport there together?

"Go," he told me. "Shivani will take good care of you. I need to wait for all the humans to be out of here first. Once they're all safe, I'll be right behind you."

"If you're waiting for the rest of them to go, then I'm waiting, too," I said. He opened his mouth—likely to tell me to get to safety—but I continued before he could say a word. "I've been waiting to see you again for days. Don't try to fight me on this."

I stared him down, daring him to do otherwise. We'd just figured out that my gift was my stubbornness. It might not be the most useful gift out of all the gifted humans here, but I was going to use it to my advantage.

Plus, Noah and I were imprinted. I could feel his desire to keep me close ebbing from the imprint bond— it was as strong as my desire to stay by his side.

I had this.

"Fine." He sighed, not looking upset in the slightest, and turned to face the witch. "Get the others first. Raven and I will go once they're safe."

She nodded and hurried over to the human closest to me. Suzanne. The older woman who'd welcomed me to the bunker when I'd first arrived gave me a small smile. Suzanne took the witch's hand and disappeared into the ether.

"Thanks." I squeezed Noah's hands and looked up into his stormy dark eyes. I wanted to kiss him again. The pull between us was so strong—like a magnet connecting his soul to mine.

"There's nothing to thank me for," he said. "After what we just went through, I'm never leaving your side again."

Even though so many people surrounded us, I stood up onto my toes and pressed my lips to his. He met me halfway, and as we kissed, my soul felt whole again.

How could I have gone my entire life without Noah in it?

We were interrupted by someone loudly clearing her throat beside us.

I reluctantly pulled away from Noah—although we kept our hands clasped together—and turned to see who wanted our attention.

It was the witch who had come with him for the

rescue mission. She wore tight, all-black clothing, and black boots with killer heels. The shoes looked impossible to fight in. But she'd proven otherwise by helping Noah take down the demon guards and freeing us from the bunker.

"We haven't had a chance to properly meet yet." She held out a hand. "I'm Bella Devereux, of the Devereux witch circle."

I took her hand and gave it a shake—her grip was firm. "Raven," I replied. "I met your sister Amber when she tracked down a demon for Noah. It was right after…" I was about to say it was right after Azazel had killed one of her sisters, but stopped myself before saying something insensitive. "It was right after Azazel attacked your circle."

"You mean after he killed Whitney." Bella's eyes darkened when she said her sister's name.

"Yeah." I nodded, unsure what more to say. I'd never been good in situations like this. Probably because I'd never experienced the loss of a loved one myself. So I went with the basic, clichéd reply. "I'm so sorry for your loss."

"Not your fault," she said. "It was Azazel's fault. And he's going to pay." She clenched her fists, fire in her eyes as she spoke.

I liked her instantly.

"Yes, he will," I agreed.

I'd originally only been part of this to help get my mom back home safely. But now it was so much more. Azazel had hurt so many people—and he planned on hurting many more. He'd taken me and locked me in this bunker. He'd taken my mom, Sage, and so many others to places we didn't know. I didn't even want to think about what he might be doing to them there.

I wasn't going to let him get away with this.

Which was why after we made sure the gifted humans were safe at the Haven, I was going with Noah to Avalon. There, I'd train to become a Nephilim.

Once I was a Nephilim, I'd have the supernatural strength to help fight in this war against the demons.

It didn't take long for the witches to transport all the other gifted humans—plus Cassandra's body—to the Haven. Once they were all gone, the witch from earlier approached me. Shivani.

She, Noah, Bella, and myself were the only ones left in the bunker cafeteria. It was eerily quiet. Half-eaten trays of food remained on the table. Many had been disturbed during the fight, so food and drinks were spilled out all over the floor, too.

It looked like there'd just been a massive food fight.

Except for the puddle of blood where Cassandra's

body had been. And the four piles of ash in various areas on the floor.

The remains of the demons.

"The four of us will teleport to the Haven together," Shivani said, holding out her hands. Bella did the same.

Noah and I took their hands, the group of us standing together in a circle.

"Ready?" Bella asked.

"Ready," Noah and I said at the same time.

The world faded around me, my stomach dropped, and in a single flash, everything went dark.

RAVEN

We teleported into the lobby of a five star hotel. It was gorgeous, with bright woven columns, intricate tiled floors, huge crystal chandeliers, and colorful seating all around.

The others were all there, standing around and staring in awe as they chatted amongst themselves. The Haven witches—the ones in all white—congregated together in the front.

Other than the color, their white outfits weren't all that different from the blue prison suits all of us humans were wearing.

Besides Shivani, who was still in our circle, only one Haven witch wasn't standing with the main group. She was off to the side with Thomas, who was holding

Cassandra's body in his arms. The two of them had their heads close together as they talked between themselves.

"The witch is promising a funeral pyre for Cassandra once we're settled in," Noah whispered in my ear. He was able to hear the conversation, thanks to his supernatural shifter hearing. "Cassandra will be honored as a noble warrior."

"Good," I said, leaving it at that. Nothing could get across the hollowness in my chest at the knowledge that Cassandra—a witch I barely knew—was killed fighting to free me and the other humans in the bunker.

The guilt weighed on me like crazy.

Noah simply wrapped his arm around my shoulders and pulled me closer. I knew through the imprint bond that he knew what I was feeling. Standing there together, we grieved Cassandra's loss.

Eventually, Thomas placed Cassandra's body into the witch's arms. The witch then walked the corpse out of the room. Thomas stared blankly at them as he watched them go. His eyes looked so pained and empty. I wished there was something I could do for him.

Sage needed to hurry up and get here. She'd know what to do.

"Where's Sage?" I looked around the lobby, trying to find her. I wasn't sure what had happened to her after

Azazel had teleported away with her, but I'd hoped she'd be at the Haven, too.

Dread settled in my stomach at the realization that she was nowhere to be found.

"She's at the Montgomery compound." Noah sounded upset—like Sage being back home with her pack was a bad thing.

I studied him, trying to figure out what was going on. "What aren't you telling me?" I asked.

"It's a long story." He glanced over at Thomas, his eyes shining with regret. "I'll tell you everything later, in private."

As he was saying it, the chatting around us quieted. I looked around to see what was going on.

A tall woman had entered the building, and all eyes were on her. She wore the same white yoga outfit as the witches who had rescued us from the bunker. Her hair was twisted up into a practical bun, her expression serene as she gazed around the crowd.

We all looked to her, waiting for her to speak.

"I'm Mary—the leader of the Haven." Her voice was warm and steady, like music. "Welcome to our home."

Her eyes stopped when they met mine, and I froze. She looked so familiar. I couldn't put my finger on it, but I could have sworn I'd seen her before.

From the way she was looking at me, it seemed like she recognized me, too.

The recognition was gone nearly as quickly as it had appeared. She looked away from me, continuing to browse the crowd with interest.

But I knew what I saw. She knew me. I wasn't sure how, but she did.

I felt like I knew her, too. And that my experience with her hadn't been good.

Noah must have sensed my tension, because he gently squeezed my hand. "Relax," he murmured, quiet enough for only me to hear. "You're safe now."

I nodded, although my instinct told me to remain on edge and alert. So that was exactly what I was going to do.

"I've been briefed on your situation, and I'm sure you're all confused and afraid right now," Mary said, her expression warm and open.

The humans who'd been in the bunker with me nodded in confirmation. A low chatter started between them.

"What the demons did to you was horrific," Mary continued, raising her arms to stop the chatter. "But the Haven is a kingdom of peace. We're literally a haven for supernaturals. We're a place where supernaturals can come and live, as long as they agree to live by our rules. As gifted humans hunted by the demons, I'm happy to extend that same umbrella of protection to you."

The low chatter started again. There were a few smiles in the crowd, but most of them looked concerned.

"That's all well and good," someone said—Harry. He'd sat at my assigned table in the cafeteria. He was middle aged and slightly overweight, and his gift was perfect aim. "But when can we go home to our families?"

From the nods and echoes of agreement from the people surrounding him, he wasn't the only one with that question.

"Do you want to put your families in danger?" Mary answered his question with a question, staring him down in challenge.

The grunts of affirmation after Harry had spoken turned into mutters of confusion.

"Of course not." Suzanne was the one to answer—not Harry.

Harry just stood there frowning, a puzzled look on his face. Many of the others looked equally bewildered.

Not me. Given my situation—with my mom being taken by Azazel because of me—I had a pretty good feeling about where Mary was going with this.

"If you go home, the demons will search for you, and they will find you," Mary said, looking at them in warning. "So if you want to keep your families safe, you can't return to them. At least not yet."

RAVEN

There was shocked silence, followed by an explosion of outrage.

Harry was the loudest of them all. He marched to the front of the crowd, his face red with anger. He looked like he wanted to grab the nearest sharp object and throw it straight through Mary's heart.

Mary simply raised her hands in the air and watched them, waiting for them to quiet down.

"Do you mean we can never see our parents again?" a small, shy voice asked from behind Harry. I immediately recognized Kara, the young girl gifted with a perfect sense of direction. She stood next to her twin brother Keith. Both of them stared up at Mary, their wide eyes scared and lost.

"Of course not." Mary smiled, as if that were ridiculous. "Never is a long time. But I advise you to stay here until the war against the demons is over. While you're all blessed with extraordinary gifts, your strength is no match for the supernaturals. With the demons hunting your kind, it's not safe for you out there. We have spells around the Haven that will prevent them from tracking you here. But if you go back to your homes, they'll find you. They'll take you again. If your family members are also gifted, they'll take them as well. And if they aren't gifted, I doubt they'll be spared."

She paused and looked around, letting her words resonate through the crowd.

Many of them looked stunned, or bewildered, or helpless.

But I knew Mary was right.

"You've been through a shock," Mary continued. "But you're not prisoners here. The Haven doesn't force anyone to stay against his or her will."

"So we can leave now?" a man whose name I didn't remember asked.

"The Haven is located in a large mountain range in Southwest India," she said. "It's dangerous to simply walk out into the rain forest. You need to be teleported to safety. And my witches expended a lot of energy bringing you here. They need a day to rest and recharge. After that, they'll return to your homes, if it's what you wish. I advise against it, but it's not my decision to make. It's yours."

People glanced around at each other and shuffled their feet. They looked frightened and unsure.

I didn't blame them. I'd panicked when Noah and Sage had told me I couldn't return home, too.

"As I said earlier, I encourage you to stay here until the demons are defeated," Mary said. "This hotel on our property was designed to keep humans safe within the Haven. As long as you stay within the hotel boundaries, you'll be protected. But you also have two other choices." She took a deep breath, as if preparing herself and us for what was coming next. "These choices are going to be shocking, so I ask you to bear with me as I explain. I —and all of the witches from the Haven—will be available to answer any of your questions immediately following this announcement. Are you ready to hear your options?"

I tilted my head, curious about what she was going to say. Many of the others did the same, some of them saying that yes, they wanted to know. Others looked small and terrified. Keith and Kara were huddled together, shaking.

Suzanne walked over to the twins and placed a hand on each of their shoulders. They both visibly relaxed under the influence of her gift of compassion. Suzanne walked around and continued to do this to the humans who appeared most scared, until they were ready for Mary to continue.

"Thank you." Mary nodded at Suzanne in recognition.

Suzanne gave Mary a close-lipped, trusting smile. She clearly felt at ease around the leader of the Haven.

So why didn't I? The question wouldn't stop eating at me.

The more I looked at Mary, the more I felt like this wasn't the first time I'd seen her. And I was deeply suspicious about why that might be.

"Firstly, you should know that when gifted humans are turned into vampires, their gifts are magnified," Mary began. "Gifted vampires are highly valued in the Haven. They help protect our kingdom. So, one of your options is to be turned into a vampire. You'll become immortal, and will have supernatural strength."

"Will we have to drink blood?" Harry asked.

"Will the sun incinerate us?" another woman asked.

"Aren't vampires monsters?"

Similar questions were echoed in the crowd until people were talking over one another. I didn't blame them for being suspicious.

Turning into a vampire wasn't a decision that should be made lightly.

"Vampires aren't monsters." Mary spoke strongly now, overpowering the questions. Everyone silenced and looked to her. "I'm a vampire. And I hope I'm not too scary." She smiled and let out a chuckle. Some of the humans eased up, but only slightly. "I and the others will answer all of your questions in the upcoming days. But no, the sun doesn't incinerate us, although its light does burn and feel draining. Yes, we drink blood. But at the Haven, we only drink animal blood. We're the *only* vampire kingdom that survives on animal blood alone." Her eyes flickered to me for a second, as if I should already know this.

I did. But only because Noah and Sage had taught me when they'd given me my "supernatural world lessons" during our long drives. I didn't know it from her. Obviously. This was the first time I was meeting her.

She had no reason to think I knew more than the others.

"In exchange for this gift of strength and immortality, you'll promise to remain in the Haven for ten years after being changed," she continued. "After that you're free to go wherever you like."

"You said we had another option," Valerie, who was gifted with the ability to sense ghosts, asked. "What is it?" She stared up at Mary hopefully, waiting for an answer.

From my conversations with Valerie in the bunker, I suspected she was hoping the other option would get rid of her gift. She hated sensing ghosts. She said they were bitter and angry.

Becoming a vampire and having that ability magnified must have sounded like a nightmare to her.

"There's only one place in the world that's safer than the Haven," Mary said. "The island of Avalon." She gazed over the crowd confidently, as if making sure we were hanging onto her every word. We were. "Avalon is protected by the angels themselves, and is ruled by the Earth Angel Annika. She's the only angel who walks on Earth. On Avalon, she's building an army that will be strong enough to defeat the demons for good. Supernaturals all over the world are journeying to Avalon to pledge themselves to her cause. Your second choice is to go there and do the same."

"But we're not supernatural," Suzanne spoke up. "We might be gifted, but we're still human."

"Humans are welcome on Avalon, too," Mary said. "They're *needed*. Because only humans can drink from the Holy Grail to become Nephilim. And only Nephilim can kill greater demons. Without Nephilim, we cannot win this war."

"Hold up." Harry held a hand out, his eyes wide. "Did you just say the *Holy Grail*?"

"I did." Mary smiled, her eyes lighting up. "The Holy Grail is with the Earth Angel on Avalon. Once on the island, you'll enter the Angel Trials. None of us know what the trials entail, but they'll determine if you're strong enough to drink from the Grail to become a Nephilim."

Chatter buzzed through the room once more. Questions, worries, and the like. But I, of course, had no questions and nothing to think about. I was going to Avalon.

I'd gone through so much to get to this point. Noah had gone through even more.

I couldn't believe we'd get to Avalon so soon.

"It's a lot to think about, as all of the choices have risk," Mary said.

The muttering increased again. People said this wasn't fair, and that they didn't ask for any of this. I didn't blame them. When I'd been brought into all of this, I'd thought the same.

But Mary raised her hands and regained control of the room once more. "There's a buffet waiting for you in the hotel restaurant," she said. "The witches from the Haven—the ones who just helped you escape the bunker —will join you for dinner." She motioned to the witches dressed in all white, as if emphasizing how the escape wouldn't have been possible without their assistance. "I know you were rescued during a meal, so we won't be offended if you're not hungry. We simply want to sit down, break bread, and make ourselves available to answer your questions."

People's eyes immediately went to where she'd motioned the restaurant was located. Mine did, too.

"Does the food have more flavor than oatmeal, boiled chicken, and steamed rice?" a man asked from the back of the crowd.

People fidgeted and glanced behind at him, chuckling nervously at the mention of the bland food we'd been forced to eat in the bunker.

"We eat a lot of the local fair from Southwest India," Mary said with a kind smile. "Indian food is made with many tasteful spices. But we had American food made as well, since we know you were all recruited from there and are more familiar with it. We prepared quite the wide variety. I'm sure you'll find something at the buffet to fit your pallet."

It was like she'd spoken the magic words.

All talk of vampires and Avalon was pushed aside, and everyone hurried toward the restaurant.

*T*asty food sounded amazing after the bland food at the bunker.

But I reached for Noah's arm, motioning for him to stay behind.

"You're not hungry?" he asked.

"It's not that." I pulled him into a corner, not wanting anyone to overhear. He leaned closer, curious, waiting for me to continue. "I recognize Mary. I haven't met her before, but I feel like I have. And she keeps looking at me like she knows me, too." It sounded silly, but I knew what I saw and felt.

I watched Noah closely, waiting for his reaction.

"You think she knows something about your missing memories." He was quick to figure out exactly what was on my mind. Thank you, imprint bond.

"Yes," I said. "Do you think there's any way we can talk with her without so many people around?"

"You got it." He took my hand, and together, we walked to where Mary and Shivani were ushering everyone into the restaurant.

I had to nearly run to keep up with his long strides. I also got my first whiff of the food, and my mouth watered at the delicious scents.

But we'd been midway through lunch when Noah had rescued us. I could eat later. First, I had to figure out what Mary knew about my missing memories.

"Noah." Mary focused on him, barely glancing at me. "It's good to see you again. I'm glad your plan was a success."

"It's good to see you again, too." He stepped closer to me, so we were standing shoulder to shoulder. We were like a barricade in front of her. "But aren't you glad to see Raven again as well?"

She paused, although she didn't miss more than a beat as she focused on me and held out a hand. "The first human to imprint on a shifter," she said. "It's so nice to finally meet you."

Apparently Noah had caught her up on our history when they'd planned the breakout from the bunker

"This isn't the first time we're meeting." I took her

hand and shook it, not letting my gaze leave hers. "We met last winter."

Sure, I wasn't totally confident in what I was saying. I was going on feelings, not facts. But she didn't need to know that.

If she did, she might be less likely to tell me what she knew.

"That's not possible." She looked back and forth between Noah and me, looking truly confused for the first time today.

"Come on." I huffed and shook my hair over my shoulder, taking on the haughty attitude I'd seen from Princess Ana in the recordings Thomas had shown me. "You might have known me by a different name, but I know I'm not *that* forgettable."

"No." Mary paled and drew back into herself. "You're certainly not."

My heart felt like it was about to beat right out of my chest. I was right. I couldn't believe it. Well, I *could* believe it, since I was the one who had suspected it in the first place. But I couldn't believe Mary had basically admitted it.

"The three of us should speak alone." Noah glanced at where Shivani and another witch had taken over leading the group into the restaurant. Everyone was almost inside. "Surely your witches can take everything over from here."

"They can." Mary walked over to Shivani and rested her fingers on her arm to get her attention. "I need to speak to Noah and Raven alone," she said. "You're in charge until I get back. Make sure the witches take care of the humans and answer all of their questions."

"Will do." Shivani closed the door to the restaurant, leaving me, Noah, and Mary the only three left outside.

"I'll get you situated in your rooms, and we can speak there," Mary said. "Unless you intend on sharing a room?" She looked back and forth between the two of us in question.

I froze, caught completely off-guard.

"That's up to Raven." Noah looked at me with a mischievous smirk. "Would you like to share a room?"

My stomach jumped with a mix of excitement and anxiety. Back at the pool house at the Montgomery compound, he'd given me the bed and taken the couch in the living room. In the hotels while we'd been out on the demon hunt, he'd taken the sofa beds in the living rooms and let Sage and I share the king beds in the bedrooms. Even at Thomas's penthouse in the Bettencourt, he'd given me the third bedroom and stayed in the media room.

We'd yet to sleep in the same room together. And we

certainly hadn't *slept* together. The most we'd done so far was kissed.

What would he expect if we stayed in the same room? Because I was beyond inexperienced. I hadn't ever had sex before. I'd come close with an ex-boyfriend from high school, but it never felt right. He'd said he was in love with me, but I couldn't say it back.

He'd broken up with me a few weeks afterward. He'd claimed if I wasn't in love with him by then, I wasn't ever going to fall in love with him.

At the time, I'd thought he was being unfair.

Now I realized he'd been right.

Because my heart had always belonged to Noah—even before we'd met.

But I didn't want to rush things between us. Not with so many other worries weighing on my mind.

Noah must have felt my rush of emotions through the imprint bond, because he smiled down at me, like he was amused. He took my hand in his and turned to Mary. "We'll have two rooms," he told her. "Next to each other. Do you have the kind with a connecting door?"

"We do." She gave him a closed lipped smile, looking back and forth between the two of us like she knew something we didn't. "Follow me and I'll get you situated."

*M*ary brought us up the elevator to the fifth floor, which was the highest in the hotel. She said it would give us the best view of the surrounding mountains. She led us down the hall and stopped at room 405.

"Here we are." She reached for the doorknob and opened it, motioning for us to walk inside.

"No lock?" I looked at the door in question.

"The Haven is a safe kingdom," she explained. "There's no crime here. We have no need for locks."

"Oh," I said. "Okay."

It really *wasn't* okay. Not having a lock on my door weirded me out.

But I knew better than to argue with a centuries old vampire queen who was keeping me and the other humans safe when she didn't have to. Especially when I wanted information from her about my missing memories.

So I followed Noah inside the room. It was surprisingly plain. The lobby was so colorful and elaborate that I'd expected the rooms to be the same. There was nothing to complain about—the room was functional and clean. It just lacked the unique, warm, welcoming feel of the rest of the hotel.

Well, that wasn't entirely true. Because there was a balcony with floor to ceiling windows, and the lush mountains outside were divine and exotic. We had mountains in LA, but the mountains I was looking at right now had deep shades of green in them that I'd never seen in my life. They were downright magical.

Noah opened a door along the wall (it didn't have a lock, since that apparently wasn't something they did here), and it led to another room that looked exactly like mine. Connecting rooms, as promised.

"We should get started." Mary shut the main door and walked to the center of the room. "The sooner I can get back down to the restaurant, the better. So tell me— how do you remember me? Your memories were erased. I oversaw it myself."

"You're the one who erased my memories?" I stared back at her, shocked. "Why would you do that?"

"It was the Earth Angel's decision," she said. "Not mine."

"You know the Earth Angel?" I was getting more confused by the second.

Mary's eyes narrowed in suspicion. "What exactly do you remember?" she asked. "Because it doesn't sound like much."

I deflated, since she was right. Might as well come clean now. "I know my memories were erased and replaced this winter," I said. "And I know the Earth Angel transformed into my form to disguise herself as Princess Ana. Other than that, I have no idea what happened to me. Which is why I came to you. For answers."

She was silent for a few seconds, studying me. "Yet you know we've met before," she finally said. "You're either lying or not making sense."

"I'm not lying," I said, standing my ground. "I've known for months that something about my memories was off." From there, I told her everything about my missing memories and the blanks I'd filled in so far. "When I saw you, I felt that we'd met before," I finished. "The only explanation could be that we met during the time when my memories were erased."

"You shouldn't have noticed that your memories were off at all." Mary watched me closely, still looking suspicious. "It's happened occasionally, when less powerful witches create the memory potion. But the memory potion we gave you was brewed by Geneva. The most powerful witch who's ever lived."

Noah cursed from where he was standing next to me. He'd been relatively quiet this entire time, letting me tell Mary my story myself. So at this sudden outburst, I turned to him in alarm.

"What?" I asked.

"Geneva's dead," he said. "She used her Final Spell at the Battle at the Vale to close the Hell Gate. She saved us all... but in doing so, she sacrificed herself."

The weight of what he was saying fell on me like a ton of bricks. "If she's dead, she can't create an antidote pill," I realized. "Unless she created one at the same time she brewed the memory potion she gave me?" I turned back to Mary, hoping she had an antidote pill created by Geneva somewhere in the Haven.

Without an antidote pill, getting my memories back would be impossible.

"There's no antidote pill," Mary said. "I'm sorry."

All the hope whooshed out of me at once. Until now, I'd held onto the possibility that there'd be a way to get my memories back. I'd thought we would find the witch who had brewed the potion and get her to create an antidote pill.

"Maybe there's another way to reverse the potion." I looked back and forth between Mary and Noah, hoping one of them would have an answer. "There has to be another way. Right?"

"There is no other way," Mary said sadly. "You shouldn't have been able to break through Geneva's memory potion to begin with. Your ability to fight past the potion has something to do with your gift, doesn't it?"

"I'm not entirely sure." I glanced to Noah for assurance, since he'd only just guessed what my gift might be when we were reunited in the bunker. He gave me a nod, and I refocused on Mary. "But we—Noah and I—suspect my gift is my stubbornness."

Mary did something entirely unexpected—she laughed. "That's a new one," she said. "What made you think that?"

I told her everything. Knowing there was something wrong with my memories, resisting the demon that had tried entrancing me at the Pier, surviving after using a heavenly weapon, convincing the demon in the bunker to turn away while I changed, and lastly, reaching Noah through the imprint bond when we were states apart.

"She shouldn't have been able to do that," Noah added. "Imprinted shifters can only communicate with each other when they're in the same room."

"But Raven's not a shifter, is she?" Mary said.

"No." Noah looked at me proudly and gave my hand a squeeze. "She's not."

My heart warmed. Since meeting Noah and Sage, I'd thought I was weak because I was human and not supernatural. But the way Noah was looking at me now made me feel stronger than ever.

"I think you're correct about your gift," Mary said, turning to me. "Stubbornness, bullheadedness, willfulness, or whatever you want to call it. You've got fire in you, Raven Danvers. And you know how to use it to get your way."

Noah smirked after she said bullheaded. It was a word he'd used to describe me way earlier in our journey.

Personally, I thought "stubborn" was a *much* nicer way of saying it.

"After Geneva created the memory potion, I gave it to you and Susan," Mary continued. "Do you remember Susan? The other human you'd been kept with?"

A flash passed through my mind—a woman sitting hunched over in a cell, her wrists dripping with blood. But it was gone before I saw a clear picture of her face.

"Not really," I admitted, shifting back and forth on my feet. "I don't remember much. All I know is that what I *do* remember—a trip backpacking around Europe

—doesn't feel like it truly happened. Hopefully you can help me fill in the blanks."

"All I know is what Annika told me," Mary said. "She had control of Geneva's ring, and therefore, of Geneva herself. Do you know about Geneva's ring?"

"No…" I shook my head and looked to Noah, since he and Sage had been in charge of my "supernatural history" lessons.

"I gave you the basics," he said in defense. "We had a *lot* to cover. Geneva's ring didn't seem important. Especially since she's dead."

"He's right," Mary said. "The story of Geneva's ring is long. I'll save it for another day. All you need to know for now is that Annika—the Earth Angel—was working with Geneva to infiltrate the palace at the Vale. She needed to disguise herself as a vampire princess. But witches don't have the power to turn humans into vampires. So Geneva improvised by making Annika *appear* to be a vampire princess. She stole two humans and a vampire princess, locked them in a dungeon, and used their blood to make transformation potions. One for Annika, and one for herself, since she accompanied Annika to infiltrate the palace. She mixed the vampire princess blood into Annika's potion, which gave Annika the abilities of a vampire princess for twenty-four hours."

"Aren't humans not supposed to know that drinking vampire blood gives them vampire powers?" I flashed back to when Thomas had forced me into a blood oath where I promised to never tell that secret to anyone.

"We like to keep it secret," she said. "But you already knew."

"How did you know that?"

"It's one of the benefits of having many gifted vampires at the Haven." She smiled. "We know things. Anyway, where was I? Oh, right. The humans Geneva kept in the dungeon so she could brew the potions." She tilted her head, her gaze locked on mine. "One of those humans was you."

RAVEN

"*A* dungeon," I repeated, standing perfectly still as I spoke.

It should have been jarring.

But it made sense. The flashes I'd been having of a dungeon... the weird dreams. They were all adding up now.

"You remember?" Noah asked.

"Sort of," I said. "I've had flashes and dreams. Nothing concrete."

"The Earth Angel didn't know Geneva was keeping you in a dungeon," Mary said. "Once she found out, she demanded Geneva bring both of you to the Haven. She insisted on the memory potion for your own good."

"I didn't agree to the memory potion." I didn't

remember, but I didn't have to remember to know it was true. I knew myself.

I'd never agree to having my memories taken away from me.

"You didn't," Mary confirmed. "I compelled you and Susan to drink it. Susan drank the potion without a fight. You, on the other hand, weren't so complacent. You tried fighting my compulsion. It was unprecedented, because humans aren't aware when they're being compelled. They certainly aren't able to try fighting it. You weren't able to fight it, of course—my powers are strong—but you were aware of what I was doing. I should have realized you were gifted right then and there."

"But you didn't," I said hollowly. "You shipped me back home. You let me believe I'd been backpacking through Europe, when I'd actually been kidnapped by a dark witch and locked in a dungeon."

"Geneva could do both dark and light magic," Mary corrected me. "She was equally strong on both sides, which is incredibly rare. It was why she was so powerful."

"Whatever," I mumbled. "That's not the point."

"It's not," Mary agreed. "The point is that you have a decision to make. Do you want to go to Avalon? Or do you want to stay here? You're gifted, and you show strong potential. I'll turn you into vampire myself. You wouldn't just be a regular vampire. You'd be a vampire princess."

Her eyes gleamed, like she expected me to say yes on the spot.

I didn't. Because sure, being a vampire princess would have its perks. I'd have strength, immortality, and I'd be able to use compulsion. Not like I'd actually *use* compulsion. I'd had my memories toyed with enough that I'd never want to play around with anyone else's free will like that.

But Noah was mortal. Did I really want immortality when the man I'd imprinted on—and might mate with— would eventually grow old and die?

No. Absolutely not.

"I'm going to Avalon," I said. "But thank you for the offer. I truly do appreciate it."

After all, Mary was a powerful vampire queen. I didn't want her to think I was ungrateful. She wasn't someone I wanted on my bad side.

"I'm disappointed you won't be staying here, but I do think you'll make a great Nephilim," she said with a curt nod. "The Earth Angel will be proud to have you join her."

I didn't know about that. I had a lot of things I

needed to say to the Earth Angel about her decision to erase my memories, and none of them were nice.

But I'd deal with that once I got to Avalon.

"I have to go through the Angel Trials to save my mom," I explained, hoping to help her understand why I'd rejected her offer. "Rosella told me that when Noah and I met with her on the Pier."

Just then, the door creaked open and a familiar, white gaze stared in my general direction. "Speaking of me," Rosella said with a knowing smile. "I thought it was about time I dropped by to say hello."

THOMAS

$\mathcal{B}$ ella and I didn't need to sit in on the question and answer session the gifted humans were having with the witches of the Haven.

We had other matters to attend to.

Matters named Dr. Foster.

A tiger shifter named Sanjay took the doctor's wrist and led us to the holding room he'd stay in while at the Haven. Sanjay was in his human form, but he shifted his fingernails into claws, warning Dr. Foster not to try anything.

Dr. Foster tried nothing, He was such a typical male witch. Weak in comparison to his female counterparts.

Male witches really got the short sticks in the supernatural world.

I didn't know what Dr. Foster was doing with those

demons in that bunker. All I knew was that the Foster witches were helping the demons. They were the reason why Sage had been bound to Azazel. Now Dr. Foster was one of the reasons why Cassandra was dead.

He was going to pay.

But first, I was going to avenge Cassandra's death. I was going to get Sage turned back to normal.

To do that, I needed information.

Dr. Foster likely *had* that information.

Which meant he was in for a rough night. Because I wouldn't rest until I knew everything he did.

We marched into the main building where Haven residents congregated to eat meals, trade goods, and spend time together. Like all of the public buildings in the Haven, it was glamorous and colorful, both inside and out.

Beautiful public spaces and minimalist private spaces encouraged residents of the Haven to spend as much time together as possible. It was empty now, due to the late hour. But it was normally bustling with people.

Sanjay eventually led us into a room in the back of the building. I knew this room. Bright, welcoming, and colorful, it was where the Haven entertained visiting guests. It was even set up like it was ready for teatime.

"Don't you have a more suitable place for prisoners?" I sneered as I looked around the room.

"The Haven is a kingdom of peace," Sanjay answered. Not a muscle in his face moved as he spoke.

I couldn't help noticing Bella roll her eyes. Rightfully so. Tiger shifters were always so catty.

"We don't keep anyone here against his or her will," he continued. "However, this is a special case, so Mary has deemed the meeting room as the appropriate place to house Dr. Foster during his stay with us. This room has extra strong boundary spells around it, in case any of our visitors get... worked up during their time here."

I nodded, since I knew from my time living here that a fair share of fights had broken out in this room. Usually the leaders who visited the Haven to broker deals in neutral territory handled themselves with decorum. But not always.

It was better to be safe than sorry when it came to supernaturals. Even weak, old, male witches like Dr. Foster.

"We'll be questioning Dr. Foster privately," I informed Sanjay. "I trust the room will be guarded while he's here?"

"Myself and another tiger shifter will be patrolling," he assured us. "Like you, we wish for no trouble in the Haven."

I nodded, trusting the man at his word. "Very well. You may leave now."

Sanjay gave a slight bow and left the room.

Once the door clicked shut behind him, I glanced over at Dr. Foster. The man had backed into a corner and was quivering in his boots.

He was right to be afraid. Especially since Bella and I still hadn't cleaned ourselves up after the fight with the demons in the bunker. We were covered in their blood.

Not just their blood. Cassandra's blood too.

I walked to the wall and brushed my finger against the light switch. Immediately, an image of all of the electronics in the room filled my head, my body buzzing as I connected to the energy emanating from them. There were cameras, of course. The Haven was the safest kingdom in the world, but even they needed cameras.

I shut them off with a single thought.

Mary and the others at the Haven would never agree to the techniques Bella and I were about to use to acquire information from Dr. Foster. But I knew Mary well enough to know that in this circumstance, she'd happily turn the other cheek.

She couldn't be responsible for something she knew nothing about.

"Cameras are down," I told Bella. "What's the status on the magical barrier?"

I didn't know for sure there was a magical barrier up.

Only witches could sense magic. But I assumed there was.

"There's one in place." She spoke slowly, concentrating hard on the room around her. A few seconds later, her eyes zoomed back into focus. "A permanent light magic boundary spell keeping all conversations in this room safe from eavesdropping."

"Wonderful." I nodded and turned back to Dr. Foster. He was still cowering in the corner. "Would you like to take a seat, Dr. Foster?" I asked with a purposefully chilling smile. "Because it's time for you to share everything you know."

THOMAS

"*I* can't tell you anything." Dr. Foster's voice shook as he spoke. "What I told you back in the bunker is true. The Foster circle doesn't exist anymore. I was kidnapped by the demons, just like those humans. I don't want any part of this. I just want to get out of here. Please."

"Pathetic." Bella rolled her eyes again and whipped out her longsword. She examined it, as if imagining everything she could do with it. "You're already a part of this. You know it as much as we do. But don't worry. We'll get you to talk."

"Easily." I smirked, since I held the trump card here. Focusing on my vampire prince abilities, I called forth magic into my tone and locked my gaze with Dr. Foster's. "Take a seat on that couch."

Dr. Foster didn't budge.

"Interesting," I said, turning back to Bella. "Check him for wormwood."

She frisked the doctor, using her sense of smell to assist her. As a vampire, I couldn't detect the scent of wormwood. It was invisible to us. But witches could smell it.

She backed away from him, irritation flicking in her eyes. "Nothing," she said. "The Foster witches must have done something to him. Some kind of spell to make him resistant to compulsion."

"Have you ever heard of such a spell?" I asked. Because I certainly hadn't.

"No," she said. "But the Fosters are one of the most ancient circles in the world. They've created spells and potions that no one else has ever heard of."

"Very well, then." I also reached for my weapon—a dagger—and toyed with it. "Looks like we'll be doing this the hard way."

Dr. Foster backed up further so he was pressed to the wall, his eyes wide in terror. "Please, don't," he begged.

I whizzed toward him and pressed the dagger into his neck. "We know about the binding spell the demons are creating with the shifters," I told him. "Now we need to know how to break it."

Confusion passed over the doctor's eyes. "I thought you wanted to know what the demons wanted with the gifted humans?" he asked.

"We'll get to that," I said. "But first, the blood binding spell."

"I can't tell you about that," he said.

I moved away my knife, lifted my leg, and whammed it straight into his old wrinkly jewels. He made an *oof* sound and bent over, his face twisted in pain as he cradled his balls.

With him in that position, I easily picked him up and threw him down onto the couch.

Now he was where I'd originally wanted him. Much better.

"Can't?" I asked, towering over him. "Or won't?"

"I can't tell you what I don't know." He didn't meet my eyes when he spoke.

Liar.

I circled him like a hawk, knife in hand. "You know one of the most painful sensations that exists?" I asked, continuing before he had a chance to answer. "Getting your fingernails ripped off. One by one. Then toenails. And then, if that isn't enough, there are certain fingers and toes that aren't needed to survive. Do you want to find out which fingers and toes those are, Dr. Foster?"

He whimpered like a pathetic animal.

I might have felt bad, if he didn't deserve it. Because he was a liar. He knew how to save Sage, and he was keeping the information from me.

I wouldn't stand for it.

"But don't worry," I said. "Once you tell us everything we need to know, Bella can acquire you some healing potion and fix you right up. Can't you, Bella?"

She eyed him up, looking as distant, disgusted, and angry as I felt. I couldn't blame her. Along with taking the humans and binding shifters to himself, Azazel had killed one of her sisters. She wanted Azazel and his accomplices—including Dr. Foster—to pay as much as I did.

"I could." She shrugged. "But to save us time—and a mess—I've got a simpler solution."

"Oh yeah?" I tilted my head, curious. "What's that?"

She reached into her weapons belt, her eyes glimmering with mischief as she pulled out a vial of dark blue potion that I was starting to recognize well.

Complacent potion.

"This," she said.

Irritation flickered through me at the sight of the potion, but I reigned it in. "You said you used all of your complacent potion when we fought Abaddon's Locust," I reminded her.

"I lied," she said. "I always like to have extra on me. For times like these." She gave me a knowing smile, aware that it wasn't an offer I could refuse.

I just stared at her, showing no emotion. I was good at holding in anger. I'd always been good at it, even before being turned. And I hated being lied to.

I also wasn't stupid enough to turn down something that could help me. So I noted for the future that Bella could be a bit of a loose cannon. A useful loose cannon, but a loose cannon nonetheless.

"All right," I agreed. "I suppose complacent potion is the most logical option."

"Stupid witch," Dr. Foster muttered from the couch.

"Stupid?" Bella raised an eyebrow, threw back her head, and laughed. "I'm not the one who's caught and captured. You're the stupid one here. Not me."

"I meant you're stupid for bringing complacent potion here of all places," he said. "The Haven follows the laws of the vampire kingdoms. Complacent potion is illegal. You know it as well as I. If you're caught with it, they'll eradicate your magic."

"No one will believe the word of a Foster witch over mine." Bella stuck her chin up, not appearing intimidated in the slightest. "Plus, I've got an antidote tablet. Once we're done with you, there won't be any trace of the complacent potion at all."

"And no one knows what's going on in here," I reminded him. "Remember? I turned the cameras off. It's just the three of us now. Alone. And we can do whatever we want to you."

His eyes widened as the true realization of his predicament set in.

I nodded to Bella to proceed.

"I don't think he's stupid enough to think he can beat you in a fight," Bella said to me. "But hold him down."

I walked over to the doctor, placed my hands on his shoulders, and held him in place. He was so weak. So pliable. His entire body shook under my grip.

The man never stood a chance.

Bella marched up to him, uncapped the needle, and sank it into his throat. He stopped shaking immediately.

Satisfied that he was under our control, I removed my hands from his shoulders and walked around him, joining Bella to face him. "Now," I said, ready to get down to business. "Tell us how to reverse the spell between Azazel and his blood bound shifters."

Dr. Foster glared at us and pursed his lips together, but the potion forced him to speak. "There's no way to reverse the spell." Now that he was fully given into the potion, he smiled, seeming to enjoy telling us this. "It has to be broken. And the only way to break it is by killing the master the slaves are bound to."

"Azazel," I muttered.

"Yes," he said. "To break this particular blood binding spell, you must kill Azazel."

RAVEN

"*R*osella!" I smiled at her familiar face, happy to see her.

The gifted vampire greeted us, shining with goodness. Simply being in her presence made me feel safe. She was radiant, even dressed in the boring white yoga outfit of the Haven. I supposed that was what happened when someone was turned into an immortal while still a teenager.

Mary looked back and forth between us. "I've told you everything I know, and I've laid your choice out for you," she said to me. "Now, if you'll excuse me, I need to return to our guests. The gifted humans surely have many questions. It's my job as the leader of the Haven to ease them into their new lives, whether that be here at the Haven, getting them safe passage to Avalon, or getting them home."

"Hopefully they choose one of the first two options," Noah said.

"I agree," Mary said solemnly. "For their sakes, and for their families."

"Go help them," I said. "And thank you. For offering us a safe haven here, and for everything you've told me."

"I doubt this is the last I'll be seeing of you, Raven Danvers," she said. "You're destined for greatness. I know it."

"You're a psychic now too?" I raised an eyebrow, surprised.

"No, no." She chuckled. "It's just a hunch. I've been around for a few centuries. After so much time on Earth, one tends to pick up on these things."

"It's a good hunch," Rosella confirmed, giving me a wink.

I didn't think blind people winked, but Rosella totally just had.

Mary excused herself and exited the room, leaving Noah and me alone with Rosella.

Rosella got situated on one of the chairs that overlooked the balcony window. "You've had quite the journey so far," she said. "But I'm happy everything is working out so well between you two."

"What do you mean?" My cheeks heated, and I glanced at Noah self-consciously.

"The imprint bond." Rosella chuckled, like I was silly for not immediately knowing that was what she was referring to.

I supposed I *was* being silly. After all, she was a psychic. She knew these sorts of things.

Which meant she also might have answers.

Excited energy jolted through me. Ever since Noah and I had imprinted, I'd had so many questions.

Rosella must have known I needed to speak to her. That must have been why she came here right now, when we had time to talk.

"You knew we were going to imprint," I realized. "Back when we first came to see you on the Pier. That's why you told us to go on the demon hunt together. Isn't it?"

Noah raised an eyebrow, apparently putting it all together at the same time as I was saying it out loud.

"I'm happy to answer your questions." Rosella held a hand up for me to slow down. "But one at a time, please."

I sat down on the bed and made myself comfortable. Noah did the same, taking the spot next to me. Immediately, our hands clasped together. Holding Noah's hand was becoming second nature to me. As corny as it sounded, I truly felt stronger with him. His energy buzzed perfectly with mine.

Together, we could get through anything this crazy supernatural world threw at us.

But first, I wanted to know more *about* us.

"Did you know we were going to imprint?" I asked Rosella, doing as she said and focusing on one question at a time.

"I knew that if you joined Noah on the demon hunt, there was a high probability of it happening," she said.

"And you said I needed to go on the demon hunt with Noah to prepare myself for the Angel Trials."

"Yes." She smiled. "But not just because of the imprint bond. The bond strengthens you, of course. But you've grown so much since that day we met on the Pier. You weren't ready for Avalon then. You are now."

Warmth shot through me at her statement. Pride. Rosella's belief in me meant a lot. I mean, if a psychic vampire believed I could do something, she must be right.

Right?

"But don't get over confident," she warned. "Everyone has free will. My sight shows me the future that has the highest probability of happening. It's up to you to use your free will to create the best future for yourself—and for the world."

"I'm going to Avalon to save my mom," I reminded her. "Not the world."

"I know." She sat back, leaving it at that.

Annoyingly vague, as I was getting accustomed to. And it was clear from her tone that she didn't intend on giving me any more information.

"Back to the imprint bond," Noah changed the subject. "I'm a shifter. Raven's a human. How were we able to imprint on each other?"

I moved closer to him and looked to Rosella for an answer.

"Since the Hell Gate opened, the supernatural world has been changing," Rosella began. "The universe always wants to maintain balance between good and evil. Without good, people destroy themselves. Without evil, they have nothing to fight for. It's like yin and yang—both sides are necessary to complete a full circle. The opening of the Hell Gate shifted that balance. Changes in the supernatural world are how the universe is reacting to move the balance back to its natural state."

I stared at her, taking it all in. "So Noah and I imprinting on each other will help... rebalance the universe?"

How could we—two people in a world of billions—matter that much?

"My sight has shown me that it's not just you and

Noah who are experiencing these changes," she said. "There are others as well." She looked to Noah, as if he might have the answer.

"Sage and Thomas," he said instantly. "They imprinted on each other, too."

RAVEN

"What?" I turned to him, both shocked and happy at the same time. "You never told me that."

"Didn't have time." He shrugged. "We've been a bit busy since I rescued you from that bunker."

"True," I supposed. He'd also told me he was going to tell me what had happened to Sage. I was worried for her. Terrified, actually.

If she were dead, he'd have told me. Right?

Of course he would have. And I would have felt his grief through the imprint bond.

So at least I knew Sage wasn't dead. I'd become close to her since she'd helped Noah rescue me from Azazel. I might even go as far as saying she was the sister I'd never had. And we were only just getting to know each other. Losing her now would be devastating.

But she wasn't here, either. Which was worrying.

I also didn't know how long Rosella had with us, and she was finally giving me answers about the imprinting. This was something I'd wanted to know for a long time.

I needed to focus on one thing at a time.

Focusing on one thing at a time was the only way I was getting through life right now. If I tried to think about everything at once, I was pretty sure I'd lose myself in a deep hole of anxiety and fear.

"So something happened to me and Thomas to make us able to imprint on shifters?" I asked Rosella.

"Not just you and Thomas," she said with another knowing smile. "The entire imprint bond process as a whole has changed. You see, for centuries the supernatural community has stayed pretty divided by species. The vampire kingdoms, the wolf packs, and the witch circles like living with their own kind. Yes, there are exceptions, like we have at the Haven. But even here, species tend to stick together. Now supernaturals need to come together to fight against the demons. And what's the best way to bring people together?"

She paused to look at Noah and me, waiting for an answer.

"A common enemy?" I guessed.

"Yes," she said. "But something else is stronger than that. Love."

"So it's not just me and Noah, or Sage and Thomas." I sucked in a breath, endless possibilities rushing through my mind. "Shifters can now imprint on *anyone?*"

"So it seems," Rosella confirmed.

"Wow." Noah sat back, shocked. "That's… different."

"You're unhappy about it?" I moved slightly away from him, unable to help feeling hurt. This change was what had allowed him and I to imprint on each other. Shouldn't he be grateful?

Unless he was going back to all that crap he'd spewed back in Thomas's penthouse about how it would be "better for me" to have a "normal relationship" instead of mating with a wolf shifter. He better not be going back to that.

Because no one was the boss of me. As long as he wanted to be with me, I could decide for myself if I wanted to be with him.

"No." He shook his head and pulled me closer, reassuring me that it wasn't what I thought.

It made me feel better, but I was still confused.

"So why do you sound disappointed?" I asked.

"I'm not disappointed," he said. "You just have to understand. In the supernatural world, things have been the same way for hundreds—sometimes *thousands*—of years. A shift like this is huge. It changes everything I've ever known. Everything my *ancestors* have ever known."

"I think that's the point," I said. "Like Rosella said, we need a shift if we want to beat the demons. This evolution in imprinting is the shift the universe knows we need to help us win."

"Apparently so," he said. "I know I'm not always the best at expressing how I feel, but I'm happy about this change. How could I not be? It brought us together. So don't you ever think otherwise. Okay?"

I just stared up at him with love and nodded. If Rosella weren't sitting a few feet away watching, I would have kissed him.

From the heat rushing through Noah's deep brown eyes, I knew he wanted the same exact thing.

But we both managed to restrain ourselves. Because sure, the seer was blind. But she'd totally know what we were up to. And that would just be weird.

"Well, it seems I've overstayed my welcome." Rosella pulled herself up from her chair. "It's best I see myself out now."

"No." I sat upright, not wanting her to leave. Well, I did sort of want her to leave so I could have alone time with Noah. But the seer had knowledge and answers. I wanted to know everything she knew. I couldn't let her walk away so easily.

"Yes," she said. "Thomas is coming up to tell you both something very important. He'll be here soon. It's a conversation best for the three of you to have alone, without me present."

"Does it have to do with Sage?" I asked.

Noah tensed up next to me. He was just as curious.

"It does," Rosella confirmed. "You'll want to hear it. And before I go…" She paused and turned her glassy eyes in my direction, seriousness taking over her features. "I wish you the best of luck in the Angel Trials. It's not going to be easy. But whatever you learn when you get to Avalon—no matter how hopeless or impossible things might seem—you must always believe in yourself. You have a gift, Raven. When you put your mind to something, you can accomplish anything. Don't ever forget that."

"I won't," I said, although breathlessness clawed at my chest.

Everyone kept telling me to believe in myself—that I could do things others couldn't because of my stubbornness.

It made me scared about whatever I was going to face when I got to that island. Because sure, I was stubborn. But I was still human. And I didn't feel ready for any of this.

But I had to be. Not just for myself, but for my mom.

For Noah. For all those gifted humans who'd been trapped in that bunker. For everyone in jeopardy from the demons who wanted to take over the world.

I just hoped I was enough.

Because I sure didn't feel like it.

Someone knocked on the door exactly a minute after Rosella left the hotel room.

"Thomas," Noah said his name loudly. "Come in."

Thomas marched inside, wearing his suit covered in Cassandra's blood. His eyes raged with determination. And he didn't comment on Noah's knowing he was the one at the door.

Probably because thanks to Noah's supernatural sense of smell, he would have known it was Thomas even if Rosella hadn't told us.

"What's going on?" I sat forward, ready to hear about Sage.

"Bella and I just had an educating chat with Dr. Foster," he said. "To save Sage, we have to kill Azazel."

"Save her?" I looked back and forth between Thomas

and Noah in confusion. "I don't know what *happened* to her. One moment Azazel had both of us in the bunker. The next, he threw me in with the other gifted humans and teleported away with Sage. That was the last I saw of her."

"We learned a lot when we were searching for both of you," Noah said.

From there, he continued on to tell me everything he and Thomas had learned and gone through with Sage while they were planning their rescue mission for me.

Dread filled my heart as I listened to the story.

"So you're saying Sage isn't Sage anymore?" I pressed my lips together, praying I was wrong.

"Blood binding to Azazel took away her free will," Thomas said. "I saw her. It was…" He paused, his eyes far off, and shuddered. "She can't stay that way. I won't allow it."

"She won't," I promised. "We're heading to Avalon tomorrow. Once we're there, we just need to get one of the Nephilim—or the Earth Angel herself—to kill Azazel." It was all we *could* do, since only a Nephilim or the Earth Angel had the power to kill a greater demon.

"True." Noah shuffled on the bed, not looking at either of us. "Except there's one small problem with that plan."

"What's that?" I asked.

"Demon teeth." He looked straight at me. "I need ten of them to get to Avalon. The demon in Chicago was supposed to be our final one. But you know how that turned out."

I nodded, since that demon ended up being Azazel in disguise, abducting Sage and me. Needless to say, his tooth wasn't acquired on that mission.

"Well, it's a good thing *one* of us can keep a level head during a crisis," I said, shooting him what I hoped was a mysterious smile.

"What do you mean?" He scrunched his eyebrows together, looking genuinely confused.

"I mean that while you were fiercely and invisibly killing demons in that bunker, I realized how important their teeth would be." I reached into the pocket of the bunker jumpsuit I was still wearing and pulled out a pointed, yellowed tooth. "So here you go. One demon tooth. The final one to your collection of ten. Just what the Earth Angel asked for."

He looked from me to the tooth and then back to me again. "Have I told you yet that I love you?" he asked.

"You might have said it back when you rescued me in the bunker." My cheeks flushed, still not used to those words coming from his mouth. "But trust me, I'll never get sick of hearing it."

He took the tooth from my hand, his skin brushing

my palm in the process. Jolts of electricity tingled through my skin at the contact.

"You're going to be the best Nephilim the world has ever seen," he said.

"You think so?" I tilted my head. I hoped he was right, but I was still so unsure of myself.

Before he could answer, someone cleared his throat. Loudly.

Thomas.

I pulled back from Noah, ashamed. Here we were, together, imprinted on each other, and telling each other how much we loved each other. It was hard not to get so wrapped up in him. But we were being completely insensitive to Thomas's situation with Sage.

Thomas might want everyone to think he was as hard as his machines and that he had no feelings. But I knew better. Sage was his world. It was written all over his face with the way he was wistfully watching us.

"Sorry," I said, lowering my gaze. "And thank you too —for helping Noah save me and the other humans in that bunker. I know that must have been hard, since you probably wanted to save Sage first. But we're going to Avalon, and we're going to save her. She's like family to Noah, and now she's like family to me. I promise we won't let her—or you—down. We're going to get her back. She's going to be okay."

The more I said it and made myself believe it, the more I hoped it would become true. That was my gift, right?

"Of course she'll be okay," Thomas said. "But in the meantime, I have to see if there's anything I can do to help prepare Cassandra's funeral pyre. I'll see both of you tomorrow." He turned and swiftly exited the room, not giving us a chance to get in another word.

The door clicked shut behind him.

I faced Noah, my heart hammering in my chest at the realization that we were alone—truly alone—for the first time since he'd rescued me from that bunker.

"I want you to stay with me tonight," I said quickly, before I lost my nerve. "If you want to, of course."

"Of course I want to," he said with a chuckle. "But Raven…" He paused and gazed down at me, troubled.

"What?" I frowned, worried I'd said something wrong.

"Mating is a major decision." He shifted, looking uncomfortable. "It's not something to be taken lightly. And after everything we've been through, I *do* want to mate with you. God help me, because like I told you before, if anything happens to me, you'll never be able to find love again. But when Azazel took you… when I thought there was a chance you might not make it…" He paused, his eyes hardening. "All I felt was regret. Regret for what I'd said to you back in Thomas's penthouse, about wanting you to be with another human so you could live a normal life. I was trying to be selfless, but I can't anymore. Because I want you. Only you. I love you. And if you want me too, then trust me, I'm the last person who's going to stand in your way of making that happen."

I stared up at him and gaped. I didn't know what I'd expected him to say, but it certainly hadn't been that. A million emotions buzzed through my body. So many that I found myself totally and completely inarticulate.

But Noah was waiting for a response. Which meant I needed to get my wits back together and *respond*.

"I love you too," I said, wanting him to never doubt that. "I want to mate with you. More than anything. You've brought magic, adventure, love, and a purpose into my life that I never dreamed I could have. You're the only one for me. But mating… it's kind of like the human equivalent of marrying. Right?"

"It is," he said.

"I never imagined my mom wouldn't be at my wedding." I looked around the stark hotel room of the Haven, feeling empty inside. Yes, the mountainous scenery outside was beautiful. Many would call this a paradise—a perfect location for a wedding.

But it wouldn't be a real marriage.

It would be an elopement.

And that wasn't what I wanted.

"When I get married, I want it to be a celebration of our love," I continued. "I want the people we love celebrating with us. If we mate right now, it would feel rushed. Forced. Like we're doing it because we're too afraid we'll lose each other if we don't. But we're not going to lose each other. So yes, I want to mate with you. But I also want to wait for the right time. And that time isn't right now."

"Practical, as always," he said with a smirk.

"Hey." I smiled back and gave his bicep a friendly slap. "I thought you loved every part of me. Even the practical, logical part."

"Of course I do." He leaned forward and rested his hands on my hips, growling a bit. "But you do realize that by waiting to mate, we'll have to wait to be intimate as well. The two acts go hand in hand."

"Right." I chewed my lip. When I'd told him my feelings about mating, I hadn't been thinking about the sex part as much as the marriage part. But it looked like now was the time to address that, too. "About that. I've never done it before. I'm a virgin." I lowered my eyes, feeling my cheeks flush again. This was so embarrassing.

Twenty-one years old and still a virgin.

I didn't regret it. I'd never regret saving myself for my one true love.

Hopefully Noah saw it the same way. Saw *me* the same way.

His lips curved up into a devilish smile. "Which means you'll always and forever only be mine," he said, looking down at me with such fierce intensity that it felt like my heart stopped beating.

There were no more words that needed to be said.

I moved up to press my lips up to his, and in that moment, despite every crazy supernatural thing happening in the world that was out of my control, everything was perfect.

THOMAS

*A*fter leaving Noah and Raven alone to enjoy their reunion, I hurried downstairs to the dining hall where Mary and the witches were chatting with the humans.

I didn't envy those humans in the slightest. They had rough choices in front of them.

We all did.

The moment Shivani saw me standing in the corner, she hurried up to me and ushered me out of the room. Shivani was one of the kindest witches in the Haven. She was their head ambassador who went from kingdom to kingdom, representing Mary and being a face of peace. I'd hosted her in the Bettencourt for a fair share of gatherings.

She and Cassandra had been friends.

The moment we were out of the dining room, grief struck across her face. We sat on one of the benches, sitting in compatible silence for a few minutes. In moments like these, there was nothing that could be said. Nothing could bring Cassandra back.

It had all happened so quickly that it didn't feel real. Part of me expected that I could teleport back to the Bettencourt and Cassandra would be in her condo, prepping potions and spells with her awful pop music blaring in the background.

I'd always chided her for blasting music so loudly that she was going to blow out her eardrums.

She'd always rolled her eyes and said, "If it's too loud, you're too old."

I supposed I *was* pretty old, compared to her.

It was unfair that someone so young and full of potential had died so soon.

"Her funeral pyre needs to happen tomorrow," I said, finally breaking the silence. "Before I head off to Avalon."

"It will," Shivani said. "My most trusted apprentices are preparing her body as we speak."

I knew what she meant. They were mending Cassandra's remains as best they could to make her presentable for the ceremony.

When supernaturals sent our vessels to the Beyond,

we liked to be as intact as possible. We liked to be remembered for who we'd been while we were whole.

Not for how we'd been killed.

"She'll have a hero's send off." It was a statement, not a question. Cassandra had died a hero. She'd have the recognition she deserved.

"Yes." Shivani raised her hand to her cheek and wiped away a tear. "She will."

We were sitting there in silence when another witch —one I didn't know—approached. She didn't look a day over seventeen. She reminded me of a school child coming to a professor with a question she was embarrassed to ask.

"Riya," Shivani acknowledged the girl. "I take it you and the others are ready to return to the bunker?"

I sat forward, instantly alert. "Why are you returning to the bunker?" I asked.

"Reconnaissance," Shivani answered. "As you know, it's the job of witches to ensure the supernatural community stays hidden from humans. Cover-ups are a huge part of what we do. We need to get to that bunker before human police stumble upon it. Or worse—before the demons realize something is amiss and remove anything from the scene of the crime that will be useful for us to know."

"Of course." I nodded, since I should have realized it.

Cassandra's death was making my brain feel like it was in a fog.

I needed to snap out of it. Sitting here doing nothing wasn't helping anything. I needed to be useful.

Usefulness was what would end up saving Sage.

"Riya is training to be the head of reconnaissance missions of the Haven," Shivani continued. "Thank you for finding me, Riya. Let's go to the others and begin."

"I'm coming with you." I stood up, not intending on allowing them to tell me no.

"No." Shivani stared me down, her expression fierce. "Reconnaissance and cover ups are witches jobs."

"They are." I straightened. Now that I had a goal in mind, I felt more like myself. Cool, calm, and ready to get what I wanted. "But this was an extremely high tech bunker. Yes, witches are best suited for reconnaissance when the places are guarded with magic. But I know this bunker in and out. I studied it as I prepared to invade it. It's equipped with technology everywhere. The mission will be more efficient with me using my gift of technology to help you move through it."

"You're Thomas Bettencourt." The young witch— Riya—gaped at me like she was seeing a celebrity. "One of the gifted princes turned by Mary. The one who moved to Chicago decades ago. The one gifted with control over technology."

"In the flesh."

"He should come," Riya said, turning to Shivani. "You're always saying reconnaissance should be handled as swiftly as possible. If this bunker is as high tech as Thomas claims, his being with us *will* be helpful."

I lifted an eyebrow and stared at Shivani pointedly. The logic I'd laid out was irrefutable. She had to know that.

"Yes." Shivani sighed and motioned for Riya and I to follow her out of the hotel. "I suppose he will be."

THOMAS

Since the strongest Haven witches had used their magic to teleport the humans out of the bunker, the reconnaissance mission consisted mostly of lower level witches or witches training to build their magic and take higher rank. Shivani was able to muster up enough juice to come as well to oversee everything, but she was the strongest witch at the Haven. The others still needed their rest.

The place where the main fight had gone down—the cafeteria—looked exactly as we'd left it. Food and blood all over the place. The body of the gifted human who had been killed in the fight was graying and cold on the floor.

It was a mess, but at least the demons hadn't returned yet. And besides the obvious disaster, there was no magic in there to be dealt with. Since the dead woman was human and not supernatural, she'd be left to be discovered by the police... or whoever stumbled upon her.

Leaving the body like that was certainly disturbing. But supernaturals had our jurisdictions, and humans had theirs. We tried our best not to mix those grounds if at all possible. It was less messy that way.

The other rooms were exactly as expected from the surveillance cameras Noah, the Devereux witches, and myself had been watching before the mission. Clean and sterile, with no magical traces. The demons had done a decent job at keeping the bunker looking like a regular human fallout shelter.

Now, we stood in a room we'd dubbed "the vault." After the demons had stripped the humans of their belongings, they hadn't bothered getting rid of them. They'd apparently thrown them all into this one big closet-like area. Like dragons hoarding a trove. There were piles of clothes in one corner. But the most interesting corner held lots of trinkets. Bracelets, necklaces, rings, amulets... I even spotted a deck of tarot cards in the mix.

Most of the trinkets were junk. But I did spot two familiar items at the top of the pile—Raven's cloaking ring, and the lapis lazuli necklace she'd worn the entire time I'd known her.

I reached for both of the items and pocketed them.

Riya gave me a side-eye as I swiped the items.

"They belong to Raven," I said. "I'm going to return them to her."

"Ah." She smiled, apparently relieved to know I wasn't stealing them for myself. "The redhead imprinted on the wolf shifter."

I nodded. Gossip sure did spread fast around here.

The witches collected all of the stuff in sacks to bring back to the Haven so the humans could sort through it there. They called most of the items junk, but noted a few as legitimately magical.

Once declaring the rest of the bunker clear, we ventured upstairs to the farmhouse.

Everything was exactly as I remembered it. Down to the two vampire corpses Noah, Bella, and I had left on the kitchen floor.

They were laid up on top of one another, although one was decapitated. His empty eyes gazed out from his head next to the twisted bodies. And their blood was everywhere. The strong, metallic scent of it filled the entire room.

Riya stared down at the corpses, her eyes wide and hollow. She took a timid step backward.

If I hadn't known she'd seen the dead human woman in the cafeteria earlier, I would have guessed she'd never seen a corpse before.

Maybe it was different for her to see vampires taken down. It would make sense. Supernaturals were difficult to kill. Especially immortals like vampires. It wasn't something that ever happened in the Haven.

Shivani glanced at Riya and three of the other trainees expectantly. "You know what needs to be done," she said.

"Of course." Riya walked up to the bodies to stand where their heads were. "Please, give us room."

We all backed away as the other three trainees joined her to form a circle around the dead vampires.

Riya removed the pack from her back, unzipped it, and pulled out a bag full of dirt. She opened it, and each witch stepped up to grab a handful. Riya was the last to take a handful of her own.

Shivani took the bag and put it back inside Riya's pack. Then she reached for another object from the pack—a vial full of either invisibility potion or water. It was impossible to tell, since the two looked the same. Shivani uncapped the vial and dropped a bit of the clear liquid into the dirt each girl was holding, like she was watering a flower.

The dirt stayed visible, so the liquid appeared to be water.

Next, Shivani put away the vial, coming back around with a lighter. Starting with Riya, she lit the flame and held it above the watered dirt. At contact, the top of the dirt burst into flames.

She went around the circle, lighting up the other witches' handfuls of dirt as well. The flames danced dangerously across their faces. For the first time watching them, I felt like I was observing true witches—not apprentices.

Riya glanced around at the three other girls, her eyes fierce and ready.

They watched her, waiting for her next move.

"Earth, Water, Fire, and Air," Riya began, staring at the flaming mound in her hand. She continued chant-ing, the words now in Latin.

She said the chant once, and then the other girls joined in, their voices rising in volume as they repeated it three times.

After the third time, they each took a deep breath, raised their hands holding the dirt to their faces, and blew—hard. Bright yellow sparks flared out and joined together in the center of the circle. The magic swirled together, growing into a giant orb. Then it shot down toward the dead vampires below.

The bright yellow light engulfed the corpses. It flashed bright, filling the circle. Then, just as quickly as it appeared, it was gone.

The bodies were gone, too. Even their spilled blood was no longer there.

Their bodies had been sent to the Beyond.

So why did the room still smell like vampire blood?

I sniffed deeply, zoning in on where the scent was coming from. The refrigerator.

Not bothering to explain myself, I marched up to the fridge and pulled the door open.

Inside was a gallon and a half of blood. Not human blood.

Vampire blood.

THOMAS

"Why were the demons keeping over a gallon of vampire blood in this refrigerator?" I asked, casually glancing around at the witches in the room.

Each of them looked clueless. Rightfully so.

Because no supernaturals other than vampires knew about the benefits vampire blood had to humans. Sure, the word got out occasionally, but the secret had managed to remain pretty well contained.

Enough that all of these witches didn't know.

I was figuring out what to tell them when a woman dressed in a blue bunker suit came flying down the stairs. Not a woman—a teen. Long brown curls flew out behind her, tears rushing down her face as she half-ran, half-stumbled down to us.

I recognized her immediately. She was one of the girls in the bunker with Raven. They'd shared the same table at meals, and they'd spent a lot of their free time together.

I thought I'd seen the last of her when the demons had barged in during breakfast and dragged her away kicking and screaming.

Now here she was.

But she didn't smell human. She didn't smell supernatural, either.

She smelled like nothing.

The witches instantly went for their preferred weapons and held them out in front of them, ready to fight.

"Stop," I commanded, stepping between the witches and the girl.

They obeyed.

Probably because the girl collapsed to her knees when she reached the bottom of the stairs.

"Help me." She breathed heavily, her glassy, bruised eyes shining with fear as she looked up at me. Her skin was icier than the palest vampire. Inhuman. Like a ghost, stuck between life and death.

Because right now, that's precisely where she was.

"I'm not going to hurt you." I held out my hands to

show I wasn't holding a weapon. Hopefully that would calm her.

After all, I'd been where she was before. It wasn't a time I liked to think about. Or that I even remembered beyond a flash or two. The emptiness, the hunger... it felt like it went all the way to the marrow of the bones.

"You're okay," I said steadily. "I'm sure you're frightened right now, but you're going to be all right. You just need to come with us. We'll get you what you need."

"What exactly *does* she need?" someone whispered behind me. Riya.

"Human blood." Shivani looked down at the girl gravely. "So she can complete the transition and become a vampire."

"No." The girl kneeling before me gasped and reached for her neck. Twin pinpoints were there—where the vampire had bitten her, nearly drained her, and then injected her with venom. "I'm a human. The vampire bit me, and I thought she was going to drain me, but then I woke up..." She looked around at all of us, confused. Then something else set in—realization. Dread. "You're all part of this, aren't you?" she asked. "You're working with them. With the demons." Her voice wavered, and she wrapped her arms around herself, collapsing inward and letting out a horrifying wail.

She wasn't making much sense. But that was to be expected. No one remembered much—if anything—from the transition period. At least nothing more other than the empty, gnawing hunger that pounded down to the bones.

I'd tried describing the transition period to Sage once. She'd said it sounded like "the *worst* level of hangry."

That was when I'd first learned the term "hangry." Hungry plus angry equaled hangry. Sage said it all the time.

"We're not with the demons," I said. "We just saved all of the gifted humans who were living in that bunker *from* the demons. Including Raven. You were friends with Raven, right?"

"Raven." The girl smiled as she repeated the name. "She said she was going to get us out of there. But I was taken away before she could..." Her eyes went far off again, horror filling them.

"Raven's plan worked," I assured her. Then I glanced back at Shivani. "She needs to be teleported to the Haven. Now. Mary will help her complete the transition."

Shivani nodded and started to walk toward the girl. "What's your name?" she asked, smiling kindly.

The girl blinked a few times, as if trying to remember.

Being in transition made the brain hazy.

"Jessica," she finally said, glancing back and forth between Shivani and me. "What do you mean by 'transition?'"

"The vampire that attacked you didn't kill you," I said. "They turned you."

Her lips curled in disgust. "I don't want to be a vampire," she said. "I want to go back home to my family and be *normal* again." She scooted back toward the staircase, pulled her knees up to her chest, and gazed up at us in terror. Her entire body shook—a side effect of the hunger.

"You can't go back to being a human," Shivani told her, kneeling down to get more on her level. "You need to complete the transition within three days after being turned, or you'll die. The transition will be painless. I promise." She held out her hand, looking at Jessica to take it. "We'll take good care of you at the Haven."

"No." Jessica stared at Shivani's hand, not taking it. "I don't want to be a monster."

"What you are doesn't make you a monster." I stood straighter, staring straight at her. "Only bad choices can make you a monster."

"Thomas is right," Shivani said. "There are many

vampires living in the Haven, and the Haven is a place of peace. We keep order in the supernatural world. We protect humanity. If you come with us, you can be a part of that. You can join our family."

"Being a vampire isn't so bad," I added. "We're strong and immortal. And since you were gifted as a human, your gift will heighten as a vampire."

She stared at me like I was speaking a different language.

It was probably best to just show her.

"I was a gifted human too," I said. "I had a knack for technology. Now, I can control it." I touched the wall to connect with the electrical system in the house. My mind tapped into it instantly. From there, I made the lights blink off and back on again one after the other, like they were dancing. "Pretty cool. Right?"

"I guess it's kind of cool," she admitted with a small smile.

Good. It sounded like she was coming around.

"What's your gift?" I asked her.

"I can tell when people are lying or telling the truth," she said.

"That's a powerful gift," I said. "You'll be able to do a lot of good with it."

"You certainly will," Shivani said, looking down at Jessica in awe. "The Haven has never come across a human with such a gift before. Mary—our leader—will be so excited to meet you."

Jessica looked back and forth between Shivani and I again, sizing us up. "If I go with you, I won't be a prisoner," she said. "Right? I'll be able to leave whenever I want?"

"You won't be a prisoner," Shivani assured her. "But we'd love for you to stay. The Haven is a literal haven for all supernaturals. You'll be safe with us. I promise."

"You're telling the truth," Jessica said.

"I am," Shivani replied. "And once you're at the Haven, we'll answer all your questions and ease you through your transition. All you need to do is take my hand. I'll transport you there straightaway."

"And that's where the others from the bunker are?" she asked. "At the Haven?"

"They're there, and they're safe," I said, and she nodded.

Her gift was making this easy. Anyone else in her position probably wouldn't have believed us this quickly. But because of her gift, she knew we were being honest with her. It was refreshing, to say the least.

"For their own safety, you won't be able to see the others until you complete your transition and we see how you handle yourself around humans," I said. "Some vampires have an easier time with blood lust than others. But you truly are in the best of hands at the Haven. I was turned by Mary and eased through my transition in the Haven as well. And I turned out just fine."

She bit her lower lip and wrapped her arms around her stomach, apparently still thinking about it. "Once I complete the transition, will this awful pain go away?" she asked.

The hunger pains. Of course.

"It will," I promised.

"All right." She reached forward and took Shivani's hand, looking focused for the first time since she'd come flying down the steps. "Take me to the Haven."

NOAH

Cassandra's funeral pyre was a ceremony fit for a hero, just as Mary had promised.

It was attended by all the supernaturals of the Haven, supernaturals close to Cassandra who lived at the Bettencourt who had teleported in for the ceremony, and Raven. Since Raven had a cloaking ring that hid her scent, she was able to attend without driving the less controlled vampires of the Haven into a blood lust frenzy.

I stood near the front with Thomas, Raven, and Jessica, who had just completed her transition into a vampire. Jessica hadn't left Raven's side since the two of them were reunited.

We all wore the white pants and tops provided for us by the Haven. I didn't like dressing like everyone else. It felt like some sort of cult. But Raven had insisted I wear it, to be respectful at the funeral. So I did.

Cassandra was laid out upon the stacked logs, which had been carved with intricate designs by the witches. The swirling symbols were supposed to ease her transition into the Beyond.

Her body had been prepared beautifully. The wounds she'd suffered during her death had been magically restored. She was dressed in a purple gown that Thomas said she loved, her makeup and hair done up like a princess.

Shivani and three other of the most powerful witches in the Haven gathered around each point of the pyre to commence the ceremony.

As Thomas was the closest person there to Cassandra, he went around in the circle and lit the watered dirt each witch held in her hand on fire. As he did, his eyes glimmered with tears.

It was unnerving to see the stone cold vampire prince show vulnerability.

Once all the witches held a glowing ball of fire in their hands, Thomas rejoined our group in the front.

"Earth, Water, Fire, and Air," Shivani began, and the witches all chanted together in Latin. Once the spell was completed, they blew on the fire in their palms.

Within seconds, Cassandra and the pyre were

consumed in a swirling orb of yellow magic. The magic shot up into the sky and met with the stars above. There was a blinding flash, and Cassandra—along with the pyre she'd been resting on—was gone.

Raven squeezed my hand the entire time. I felt her nerves pulsing through the imprint bond. I'd warned her about the supernatural funeral ceremony ahead of time, so she wouldn't be alarmed. But it was still a shock to see every time.

"She's in the Beyond now," I murmured in Raven's ear. "Her body has been reunited with her soul, and she's whole again."

After explaining the funeral pyre to Raven, she'd explained to me that humans buried their dead.

I already knew that, of course. Supernaturals were aware of human customs. We found the concept of burying the dead to be strange.

How were bodies supposed to reunite with their souls in the Beyond if they were buried on Earth?

Realizing I'd become lost in my thoughts, I refocused on the funeral. People had started filtering out to return to the courtyard. There, those closest to Cassandra would sit and be greeted by everyone offering their condolences. There would also be a lot of food. That was something supernatural funerals had in common with human funerals—there was never a lack of things to eat.

Raven and I had just finished making ourselves sandwiches at the buffet when someone tapped on my shoulder.

I turned around and saw the one person I'd been hoping I *wouldn't* run into on this trip.

"Karina," I said her name, standing straighter at the sight of her.

Her dark brown hair was loose and flowing over her shoulders—a far cry from the tight, pinned up-dos she used to wear. Her green eyes sparkled, and she looked happier than ever.

I had a feeling that happiness had to do with the man standing beside her. He was only a few inches taller than she was, and kind of small for a dude. His appearance was average, at best. But his eyes gleamed with intense intelligence beyond what one even expected from the oldest of vampires. It was like he knew everything about me just from looking at me.

Whenever Karina had spoken of Peter, it had always been about his mind. That was what had drawn her to him during their first conversation on board that old boat she'd met him on. So I wasn't surprised that he looked smart.

"Noah." She smiled, giddy as she exchanged glances

with the man standing next to her. This was a side of her I'd never seen before. It suited her. "I'd like you to meet my husband Peter."

I held out my hand, which he took in a firm shake. "Nice to meet you," I said.

"And you," he replied. "I heard you protected Karina during the Battle at the Vale."

"We worked together," I said. "But Karina can hold her own. As I'm sure you know."

"I do." He glanced over at her with an adoring smile. When he returned his focus to me, he was serious once more. "But she was in great danger in the Vale, and you kept her safe. For that, I'm forever in your debt."

I nodded and shuffled my feet. I wasn't about to reject his offer of an alliance—it could come in handy someday. But this whole exchange was awkward. I could only assume that Karina had been honest with Peter about everything that had happened in the Vale.

Which meant he must know about the brief relationship she'd had with me. If it could even be called that.

The strangest thing was, looking at Karina and Peter together now, all I felt was happiness for them. I'd cared for Karina, yes. I'd even thought I was in love with her.

Now that I'd met Raven, I realized that I'd never been truly *in* love with Karina. Infatuated and attracted to her, sure. And I had truly cared about her.

But it hadn't been love. Of that, I was now sure.

And now that the four of us were standing next to the buffet, I realized I still hadn't introduced them to Raven. "This is Raven," I said, reaching for her waist and pulling her closer to me. "Raven, this is Karina and Peter. Like Peter said, Karina and I worked together during the Battle of the Vale. It's a long story. And Peter…" I paused, not quite sure how to drop that one on her.

"I came back from the dead," he said simply. "Or rather, Karina brought me back."

"How so?" Raven tilted her head, intrigued.

"She made a deal with a faerie."

Raven's mouth dropped open. I didn't think I'd ever seen her so surprised. And that was saying a lot, given everything thrown at her these past few weeks.

She got a hold of herself and turned to me. "You and Sage never told me about *faeries*," she said, looking like a pup seeing the Northern Lights for the first time. "They truly exist? Real, actual faeries?"

"They live in the Otherworld." I shrugged. "They don't come to Earth often."

Karina looked between Raven and me with a knowing smile. "I think we'll leave the two of you to discuss the fae," she said. "I'm thirsty, and there's a bar full of spiced animal blood calling our names. It was nice catching up with you, Noah. I'm glad to see you're doing well."

"You, too," I said, meaning it. "But one more question. Did you ever get your memories back?"

"No," she smiled wistfully. "Fae magic is stronger than anything on Earth. But it doesn't matter. True love is true love. My memories may be gone, but the feelings are still there. Peter's filling me in on the details I've forgotten."

She took Peter's hand, and together, they walked across the courtyard to the bar.

Watching them walk away felt surreal. Like an out of body experience.

If you'd asked me months ago how I'd feel seeing them together again, I wouldn't have believed I'd truly be happy for them. Back then, I didn't think I'd ever be able to see Karina without my chest hurting with the emptiness of what I'd lost with her. I didn't think I'd ever stop wishing she'd chosen me over Peter. Sure, I'd understood why she'd done it. If you love someone enough to make a deal with the fae to bring them back from the dead, you pick that person. But it still hurt. I hadn't thought it would ever *stop* hurting.

It's crazy how much can change in such a short period of time.

Raven was still looking at me, although her shock

over the fae had turned into a smirk. "Tell me I'm not going crazy," she said. "But did I just meet one of your ex-girlfriends?"

"It was never anything official," I said, leading her over to an empty table where we could eat our sandwiches. "But yes. Karina and I have a history."

I went on to tell her the basics of what had happened with Karina during her time at the Vale. It wasn't easy, but Raven deserved to know everything. We were imprinted. Besides, I had nothing to hide. Karina and I had been a thing before Raven and I had met. Now that I knew Raven, I'd never dream of looking back.

"I really am happy for her and Peter," I finished. "Especially because if Karina hadn't brought him back from the Beyond, I never would have met you."

Raven nodded, although her eyes were far off. She was focused on Karina and Peter, who were sipping from glasses of blood as they offered Thomas and the others who had come in from the Bettencourt their condolences.

"You have nothing to be jealous of." I reached for Raven's chin and forced her eyes to meet mine. "I love you. *Only* you."

"I'm not jealous." She glanced down at her hands, as if embarrassed.

"But you're not happy."

"No." She shifted in place and swallowed, clearly nervous. "It's just... Karina's a vampire who's been around for over a century. She's experienced. In ways I'm not."

It didn't take a genius—or our imprint bond—to realize she was talking about intimacy. "You and I imprinted," I said. "We're connected in a way Karina and I could never be. Besides, once we're mated, you'll get plenty of experience. I promise you that."

Raven's cheeks turned red, and I couldn't help it—I leaned forward and kissed her. Just a light peck.

I stopped myself from deepening the kiss. We *were* at a funeral, after all.

Her eyes got that dreamy look they always got whenever we kissed. But she quickly regained focus.

I could feel through our imprint bond that her worry about comparing herself to Karina had been vanquished.

"Come on." She collected our empty plates with one hand and reached for mine with the other. "We should go be with Thomas. This is the only night he has to grieve. He needs those closest to him right now... even though he won't admit it."

I followed her, since she was right. Tonight, we'd grieve Cassandra.

Tomorrow, we were off to Avalon.

RAVEN

*T*oday was the day.

I was going to Avalon.

It didn't feel real. Because I had to admit—there was a part of me that had worried I wouldn't make it through the hunt. That I'd die before being able to save my mom.

But it had been a risk I'd been willing to take. After all, she'd do the same for me.

I played with the bangles around my wrist as Noah and I took the elevator from our floor down to the lobby. The bangles had been my mom's. The witches had collected them—plus other items owned by the gifted humans—from the bunker. After returning from the reconnaissance mission, they'd laid out all the items and told us to claim what was ours.

I'd been wearing my mom's bangles since, along with my cloaking ring and lapis lazuli pendant that Thomas had personally returned to me.

Noah reached out his hand to stop me from playing with the bracelets. "It's going to be fine," he assured me.

"I'm not nervous," I said, bouncing on my feet. But who was I kidding? Of course I was nervous. And if there was anyone I could open up to, it was Noah. "Okay," I admitted. "I'm nervous."

"Really?" Noah looked at me, smirked, and raised an eyebrow. "I couldn't tell."

The elevator doors opened, and the sense of comfort I'd felt from the second before evaporated. Because last night, after Cassandra's funeral, Mary had told us that anyone who planned on going to Avalon was to meet in the lobby the next night.

Much to Noah's digress, we were fifteen minutes early. I didn't like to risk being late. Even if the meeting spot was just an elevator ride away.

Mary was already waiting there, along with Shivani and some of the other witches who would be teleporting us to the Vale. Because no one—not even the most powerful witches in the world—could teleport straight to Avalon.

Avalon's location was hidden from everyone but those who had been there before. Therefore, the vampire kingdom of the Vale acted as a "gate" for people to get to Avalon. Mary had been in touch with the king of the Vale—King Alexander—to brief him on everything that had happened with the gifted humans and our escape from the bunker. He was expecting our arrival today.

Well, he was expecting the arrival of the gifted humans who had chosen to go to Avalon. From the chatter I'd been hearing, most of my previous bunkmates were going to stay at the Haven. After speaking at length with Mary and the witches, many of them were even considering being turned into vampires.

I supposed I couldn't blame them. The Haven was safe. It had existed here in peace for centuries, and was providing us with everything we needed to survive. The airy, spacious hotel Mary had built for the humans here was quite the upgrade from the cramped bunker. And by turning into vampires, they could solidify a home here and gain the strength they needed to protect themselves —and possibly their families—in the dark times to come.

Avalon, on the other hand, was unknown. New. Risky.

It was also my destiny.

And so, I walked into the lobby with my head held high. I was ready for whatever was coming.

Hopefully the more I told myself that, the more I'd believe it.

"You're the first ones here," Mary said, as if it wasn't obvious.

"Let's hope we're not the *only* ones who will be here," Noah said. "No offense. It's just that the Earth Angel's army could probably benefit from the help of gifted humans, too."

"None taken," Mary said. "The Haven supports Avalon and the Earth Angel's efforts. If not many humans decide to come to Avalon today, they're not prisoners here. If they change their mind and decide they want to go to Avalon, our witches will gladly bring them to the Vale. They all know this."

I nodded, reading between the lines of her words. She didn't think many others would be joining us today.

She was right. Out of everyone who'd been in the bunker, only five others joined us in the lobby.

The first was Jessica, which wasn't a surprise. She'd already told me she was leaning toward going to Avalon. Plus, we'd grown attached to each other in the bunker. She felt like a younger sister to me.

It was amazing how close you could feel to someone after surviving such an extreme situation together. And while I had no idea what she must be going through after being changed into a vampire against her will, I was glad I'd be there with her as she transitioned into her new life.

Plus, it was never a bad thing to have a walking lie detector by your side. We still hadn't figured out how Jessica's ability had been enhanced by her change into a vampire, but I was looking forward to finding out.

Thomas was exactly five minutes early. Unlike the rest of us, who were wearing the comfortable white clothes supplied to us by the Haven, he was dressed in a three-piece business suit. His normal attire. He must have had one of the vampires who'd come in for Cassandra's funeral bring it from the Bettencourt. He was perfectly calm, put together, and ready to fight. Looking at him now, one would never think he was mourning someone who was like family to him.

"You sure the Bettencourt will be able to run without you?" Noah asked.

"I'm sure." Thomas nodded. "I've always known there might come a day when I wouldn't be there to run the hotel. My coven is trained in what to do in this situation. And I don't expect to be gone for long. Once Sage is rescued and the demon bond is broken, the two of us will be returning to the Bettencourt. She'll take her rightful spot as co-leader of the coven, by my side."

Noah raised an eyebrow. I could feel through the imprint bond that he doubted Sage was just going to agree to be queen—or whatever they called it—of the Bettencourt.

We'd have to see what she decided once Azazel was dead and her free will was returned to her. But I had a good feeling that whatever she and Thomas decided, they'd make the decision together.

The only three humans who joined us were Kara, Keith, and Harry. They all came down together, like a family unit. The twins were only thirteen, but they looked younger than usual next to Harry.

"Glad to see you decided to join us," I told him with a smile. "Your ability will come in handy in the Earth Angel's army."

He just cracked a nervous small smile and nodded.

"What's your ability?" Noah asked him.

"Perfect aim," he said.

"Nice."

The two of them exchanged a typical dude look of respect.

Mary glanced at her watch and looked around at the group. "So, this is it, then."

"I guess so." I looked around in disappointment. I'd thought that out of everyone from the bunker, more would want to come to Avalon. And I suppose, selfishly, I'd wanted them there because I didn't want to go through the Angel Trials alone. Yes, I'd have Noah rooting for me—and now Jessica, too. But only humans could become Nephilim. And while I didn't know much, if anything, about what The Angel Trials would entail, the twins didn't look like they'd gone through puberty yet. I doubted they'd be ready.

Which left Harry and me.

Hopefully I'd make other friends once I got to Avalon. Not like there was anything *wrong* with Harry. I was just hoping that one of the other humans closer to my age—someone I could relate to more—would have come with us. But oh well. It was what it was.

"Well, then," Mary said, looking around at all of us. "Are you all ready?"

Just as we were all saying yes, the elevator doors opened.

And Bella came running out of them.

*B*ella hurried toward us with surprising grace given her five-inch stiletto boots and tight leather pants. "I'm not too late, right?" she asked, tossing her long hair over her shoulder.

"For what?" I asked.

"Avalon," she said, like I was stupid for not realizing it.

"You're not going back to the Devereux mansion?" I asked. "To be with your sisters?"

"Ever since Azazel killed Whitney, Amber has been keeping us on lockdown in that house." Darkness crossed over Bella's eyes as she said her murdered sister's name. "I get it—I do. We have to be safe. But I've been going stir crazy in there. It's awful." She moved from foot to foot as she spoke, as if showing us how restless she was getting.

"What about Amber, Evie, and Doreen?" Noah asked. "Don't they need you?"

"The minimum number of witches a circle needs to be complete is three," Bella said. "So yes, the Devereux circle will be able to continue doing their thing without me there. I'll be more of a use against the demons in Avalon than in LA."

Shivani was listening to our entire exchange, and she looked concerned. "Have you spoken to your sisters about your decision?" she asked Bella.

"I have," Bella said. "I barely slept last night. I was too busy trying to decide what to do. I was on the phone with them for hours. When I first told them I was thinking about going to Avalon, they were angry. But the more we talked, the more they understood. Especially because they want to do whatever they can to help the Earth Angel's efforts in Avalon, but none of us have been able to get in contact with her."

"She's been out of touch with the outside world since getting to Avalon," Noah said. "She's focusing on building her army."

I didn't know how he knew that. But he sounded really sure of himself.

Noah clearly had faith in the Earth Angel. *Everyone*

who had met her did. Even those who hadn't met her had faith in her.

But I couldn't control the worry brewing deep in my gut that something wasn't right. Probably because she'd made the decision to wipe my memories.

I couldn't wait to hear what she said to me when I walked onto that island and confronted her straight on.

"Preparing humans to become Nephilim is no easy task," Mary said.

"I understand that," Bella said. "Which is why I want to be a liaison between Avalon and the Devereux circle. I'll be fully devoted to the Earth Angel and her army, of course. I'll do whatever she needs me to do on Avalon. But I can also keep my sisters informed about what we're doing on Avalon, so they can help our cause from our house in LA."

"The choice is yours," Mary said. "You don't need to defend it to me. And now that you're joining us, that's one fewer witch from the Haven who will have to transport the others to the Vale."

I glanced around at everyone standing there who would be going to Avalon. Me, Noah, Thomas, Bella, Jessica, Kara, Keith, and Harry.

The only one who didn't look nervous was Noah. And Thomas. But he never looked nervous.

"So, this is all of us, then?" I asked.

"One more will be joining you." Mary pulled out her phone, pressed a few buttons, and held it to her ear. "Bring him in," she said to whoever was on the other side of the call. "We're ready to head out."

I didn't have time to ask who she was speaking to. Because the next second, a dark skinned man with cat-like features let himself into the hotel. He was leading chained, handcuffed man wearing the white garb of the Haven. Dr. Foster.

The male witch's eyes were wide and terrified as he glanced around the hotel lobby. He looked so much smaller than the last time I'd seen him. Like the time in the Haven had aged him years, even though we'd only been here for a two days.

Finally, he focused on Mary. "What are you doing with me?" he asked. "I already told you everything I know."

"I know you have." Mary was as cool and composed as ever. "It's a shame you didn't know why Azazel and his demon followers were collecting vampire blood in that bunker. But we *will* figure it out. I promise you that."

Right—Jessica had told me all about that after she'd come to the Haven and completed her transition. The demons had been strengthening us up in the bunker to prepare us to be changed into vampires. What the demons were doing with the gifted vampires after they completed the change was unclear.

Thomas and some of the witches from the Haven who had returned to the scene of the crime believed the demons were draining the gifted vampires of their blood and using the blood for something important.

But my mom had been taken from the bunker. And Rosella had promised she was still alive. So clearly, what Thomas and the witches thought was wrong. They *had* to be wrong.

I refused to accept any other possibility.

"In the meantime," Mary continued, focused on Dr. Foster. "The Haven doesn't allow criminals to live in our kingdom, incarcerated or not. You'll be dropped off at the Vale with the others. I've spoken with King Alexander. He'll decide what to do with you once you arrive."

Dr. Foster hung his head and said nothing. I felt kind of bad for him. I knew I shouldn't, since he was a part of keeping me and the other gifted humans captive. But I still remembered the way he'd acted during my initial physical. He'd been worried and nervous. Like he didn't want to be there.

The Foster witches were supposed to be some fearsome, ancient, dark magic family. But Dr. Foster wasn't any of those things at all.

Before I could think about it further, Mary's cell phone lit up with a text.

She glanced down at it and sent a reply. Then she looked back up at us. "The Honorable Jacen Conrad, Ambassador of Avalon, is ready to meet you at the Vale," she said, her eyes serious as she focused on each of us individually. "Good luck. And safe journeys to Avalon."

We were each assigned a witch to teleport us to Avalon. Shivani took Dr. Foster, Bella took Thomas, and the rest of us were all assigned others. My witch was named Riya. She'd been on the reconnaissance mission with Thomas and Shivani. She was a few years younger than I was, but her eyes held wisdom that I knew mine didn't.

I supposed that's what happened when you grew up in a secluded supernatural vampire kingdom and had been training in magic since birth.

The witches were dropping us off in the throne room in the palace of the Vale. They'd all been there before, so there was no risk of them accidentally teleporting into the wrong spot.

I took Riya's hands. She wore rings on each finger—

so many rings that some of her fingers had two or more on them. They were all different crystals and symbols. She seemed to favor moonstone.

Moonstone had been popular in the jewelry I'd sold while working at Tarotology.

Working there felt like forever ago. A lifetime ago.

In a way, it had been.

"Are you ready?" Riya asked.

I barely had time to nod before the ground dropped from below us and we were sucked into the ether. For a few seconds, I was weightless and everything was pitch dark. Then my feet were on solid ground again, and a throne room materialized in front of me.

I gazed around my new surroundings. High ceilings, marble floors, and impressive steps leading up to two elaborate stone carved chairs. The throne room in the palace of the Vale. Thomas had shown me a recording of it when I'd been at the Bettencourt. It was the room where the Earth Angel—disguised to look like me—had marched inside and declared herself Princess Ana of the Seventh Kingdom.

Prince Jacen stood at the top of the steps, looking down at us. With his dark hair, slim build, and strong jaw, I recognized him from the recording. He was one of those people you didn't forget—especially because he'd been a rising Olympic swimmer before being turned into a vampire. But unlike in the recording, he wasn't dressed in a fancy tux.

Today, he wore black jeans and a matching t-shirt. Not what I expected from a former famous athlete, a prince of the Vale, and an ambassador of Avalon.

Also unlike in the recording, it wasn't crowded in the throne room. It was just our group from the Haven, Prince Jacen, and a few guards standing along the walls. And there were no windows anywhere. The room was a fortress. I wouldn't have been surprised if it was the safest place in the palace.

The prince's eyes locked on mine. His silver gaze was hard and in control. The eyes of a leader. But he was also looking at me like he recognized me. It made sense, since he'd known me as Princess Ana.

I instinctively stepped closer to Noah and clasped my hand in his.

Noah glared up at the prince, sending him a clear message. I was his. Don't touch. His entire body was tense with warning.

Jacen's gaze quickly moved away from mine as he focused on Shivani. "Thank you for bringing the new prospects here," he said. "Now, if the Haven witches can step aside, I'd like to address those of you wanting to go to Avalon."

The witches did as instructed. Shivani brought Dr. Foster with her, leading him by his chain.

Now only Noah, Thomas, Bella, Jessica, Kara, Keith, Harry, and I stood in the center of the vast room. Jessica stood slightly behind me, Thomas and Bella stood together, and the three other humans had gathered in a cluster.

Jacen sized us all up and walked down the steps, so we were all standing at the same level. "Welcome to the Vale," he finally said. "Other than Avalon, the Vale is one of the safest places in the world. It's right up there with the Haven, thanks to the team of strong witches upholding a powerful boundary spell around our land. The Vale is home to vampires, wolf shifters, and humans who willingly live here in exchange for donating their blood. It also serves as the gateway between Earth and Avalon. Which is why you're here today."

"You mean Avalon isn't on Earth?" I wasn't sure if we were allowed to speak to the prince yet, but the question popped out of my mouth anyway.

Hopefully I hadn't broken some sort of royal protocol.

The corner of his lips lifted into a small smirk. "Avalon exists on its own realm, although it's anchored to Earth in a variety of ways," he said. "The Vale is one of those ways. I take it you're Raven?"

"I am." I nodded, even though the answer he'd given to my question was still confusing. And he was definitely switching the topic by asking my name.

"I'm glad Mary warned me that you were the human whose blood Geneva used for the Earth Angel's transformation potion," he said. "Otherwise, I would have been in for quite the shock at the sight of the infamous Princess Ana of the Seventh Kingdom teleporting into our throne room." He smiled, clearly trying to break the ice between himself and our strange little group.

Given the romantic past he'd had with the Earth Angel while she was disguised to look like me, I didn't want to like him. I worried it would cause territorial issues between him and Noah.

But the guy standing before us wasn't the pompous, entitled vampire prince I'd expected. He seemed cool and down to Earth. Like someone you could kick back and chill with. I could picture him and Noah having a beer together while watching football, or whatever sport they preferred.

At the same time, he was poised and confident. A leader. I could see why the people of Avalon followed and respected him.

Hopefully the Earth Angel wasn't this cool and relatable, too. It would make it really hard for me to continue being angry at her for erasing my memories.

"I'm a far cry from Princess Ana of the Seventh Kingdom." I chuckled at the mere idea of myself as a haughty vampire princess. "I'm just Raven Danvers, a human from LA."

Well, I was a *gifted* human. Who'd imprinted on a wolf shifter. While trying to rescue my mom from the greater demon who'd abducted her.

Wow, my life was weird.

"You're brave to want to come to Avalon and face the Angel Trials," Jacen said, although he moved his focus away from me to study the others in the group. "All of you are brave." When his gaze landed on Noah's, he stopped, watching him carefully. "It's good to see you again, Noah," he said. "I take it you have the items the Earth Angel requires of you for your entrance to Avalon?"

"I do." Noah held his gaze with Jacen's. "All ten of them."

"Please show them to me."

Noah didn't move. "When the Earth Angel gave me the task, she said they needed to be presented to her," he said.

A dark shadow passed over Jacen's eyes. "I speak for the Earth Angel now," he said.

Dread gathered in my stomach. "She's not..." I raised a hand to my mouth, unable to say it. But everyone was looking at me, so I had to continue. "She's... still alive," I said, since it sounded better than asking if she was dead. "Right?"

"Of course." Jacen's eyebrows furrowed. He looked genuinely confused that I'd jumped to that assumption. "But she has a lot on her plate at Avalon. The two of us lead together. I'm in charge of bringing your group to Avalon, and Noah isn't permitted onto the island until he's completed his task. I'd like to get you all to Avalon as quickly as possible so... the demon teeth, please?"

There was a tug on my imprint bond. Noah was about to communicate with me.

I didn't look at him, not wanting anyone to suspect we were hiding anything.

Something's off, his message came through in my mind. Since we were still holding hands, I heard his voice loud and clear. *Annika specifically said she would be the one verifying that I'd completed the task. She said she'd be the one greeting us at the Vale.*

But Annika isn't here, I replied. *And we need to get to Avalon. Do you trust Jacen?*

Yes. Noah didn't pause to think about it.

Then show him the teeth. We'll figure out what's going on with the Earth Angel once we're on Avalon.

Noah must have agreed with me, because he let go of my hand and reached into his pockets. After fishing around in there for a few seconds, he pulled his hands out and opened his palms.

Five pointed, yellowed, disgusting demon teeth sat in each of his hands. Ten in all.

Jacen walked forward until he was right in front of Noah to study the demon teeth. He made no attempt to touch them.

I couldn't blame him. The teeth were gross. But at least they were dry now. When I'd taken that final one from the pile of demon ash in the bunker, it had been covered in saliva.

I shuddered at the memory. I really would do *anything* for Noah. Even touch a nasty, spit-covered demon tooth.

"Tell me the truth," Jacen said, looking straight at Noah. "Did you kill each of these demons with your own hand?"

"I did." Noah smirked. "And I won't hold it against you that you used compulsion on me to get me to answer honestly."

Jacen's silver eyes sharpened. "No one can hear the difference when a vampire uses compulsion," he said. "Not even a shifter. So how did you know?"

"I didn't." Noah shrugged. "I guessed. And you just confirmed I was right."

"Touché," Jacen said with a hint of a smile. Then he

turned to the rest of us. "Are you all one hundred percent certain you want to go to Avalon?" he asked.

"Yes," I answered immediately.

Most of the others answered strongly, too. Harry answered a second after the rest of us, and the twins spoke so quietly I could barely hear them. They were the only two who sounded unsure. I supposed it was to be expected, given how young they were.

Once we were on Avalon, I'd look out for them. I didn't know them well, but we'd been in the bunker together. I felt semi-responsible for them.

"Great." Jacen nodded. "Guards—escort Dr. Foster to the prison. Haven witches, you're free to teleport back home. And the eight of you." He paused, looking at the eight of us standing before him. "Follow me. You're all welcome on Avalon... as long as Avalon welcomes you."

RAVEN

"**W**hat do you mean?" I asked as Jacen led us out of the throne room and into the hall. It was the biggest hallway I'd ever seen. It had arched ceilings, elaborately carved walls, and crystal chandeliers. It reminded me of the Hall of Mirrors in Versailles.

"What do I mean by what?" Jacen didn't even glance at me over his shoulder as he strode ahead. There weren't many people in the hall, but the few who were there cleared a path for us as we continued forward.

Was Jacen serious? He had to be playing with me. Obviously he knew what I meant.

"You said we're all welcome on Avalon, as long as Avalon welcomes us," I said. "Is there some kind of application process we have to go through or something?"

Once I said it out loud, it sounded lame.

No—it sounded *human*. Application processes were for colleges and jobs. What Jacen had said sounded far more magical than that.

"You'll see." Jacen turned into a smaller hallway, led us down it, and stopped at a door at the end. The door didn't look much different from any of the other doors in the hall. In fact, it was *plainer* than the others. But he removed a key from his pocket—one of those antique, iron-woven keys that girls sometimes wore as necklaces —placed it into the keyhole, and twisted it until it clicked open.

The door creaked as it swung outward, revealing a stone staircase going deep underground. It smelled damp, musty, and humid. Strange for this high up in the mountains.

"Who wants to go first?" Jacen stood by the door, motioning for us to go ahead.

"I'll do it." Noah was quick to volunteer.

"I was kidding." Jacen stopped Noah right as he was about to step through. The two guys stood in a stand-still, their chests puffed out as they gave each other death stares. "I'm taking you to Avalon. I'll lead the way."

He made his way down the stairs, not leaving it up for debate.

I pressed my lips together to stop from chuckling. Noah and Jacen were *totally* going to be friends on Avalon.

The stairwell was so narrow that only one person could walk down at a time. Noah followed Jacen, and I was behind him. Jessica followed behind me, since she'd been glued to my side since we'd reunited in the Haven. The humans followed her, and Thomas and Bella took the rear.

Once the door closed behind us, it no longer felt like we were in a palace, but in a cave. And just like a cave, it was pitch dark inside.

Those of us with cell phones—meaning Jacen, Noah, Thomas, and Bella—used their flashlight apps to guide the way. The rest of us didn't have phones on us. The demons had taken them from the humans in the bunker and had apparently destroyed them, since they weren't among the piles of stuff returned to us. I hadn't had a cell phone since leaving my apartment with Noah and Sage the night they'd broken in and changed my life forever.

Bella chitchatted with the humans and Jessica as we continued down, and down, and down. The rest of us were pretty silent.

"How much further do these stairs go?" I asked. We'd walked so far down that we were deep into the mountain by now.

"We're about halfway there," Jacen said. "You're not getting tired. Are you?"

"No," I answered quickly, despite the fact that my chest felt tight from the altitude. After saying it, I could practically feel Jessica's eyes boring into my back from behind me.

She knew I'd lied.

"Good," Jacen said. "Getting tired now wouldn't be a good sign for how you'd fair in the Angel Trials."

Great. Just freaking great.

But I couldn't let him get to me. Rosella believed I could complete the Angel Trials. I wouldn't let a snarky vampire—and a bit of tightness in my chest from the altitude—make me doubt myself now.

I was also aware that if it weren't for us four humans, the supernaturals would be down the stairs by now. They were going at our pace for our benefit.

Maybe the Trials had already begun, and this was the first one? I was probably overthinking things. But who knew?

We continued on until finally reaching the bottom of the stairs. They dropped us off into a small cave about the size of my bedroom at home. It was a dead end.

"What now?" Noah asked exactly what I was thinking.

Jacen walked to the opposite side of the cave. "This is going to be bright," he warned. "You might want to shield your eyes."

I didn't listen. Whatever was about to happen, I wanted to watch.

The others didn't listen, either.

I supposed we were all curious. We wouldn't have chosen to go to Avalon if we weren't.

"I tried." Jacen shrugged. "Although for what it's worth, I tried watching my first time, too."

He turned around, placed his hand on the wall, and the area surrounding his hand started to glow. Yellow like the sun, the light heated my face. It got bigger and brighter until it was so intense that it burned.

Bella, Thomas, Noah, and Jessica raised their arms to guard their faces first. With their supernatural sight, the light was probably worse for them.

Finally, it got so big and bright that I had no choice— I *had* to turn around and shield my eyes. It was so hot that my skin felt like it was on fire.

The twins screamed behind me, their cries echoing across the cavern walls. The pure terror in their screams rattled me down to my bones.

Noah's arms wrapped around me, as if he could

protect me from the burning light. *I love you*, he said through the imprint bond. *Whether we mate here or in the Beyond, my heart will always be yours.*

And mine yours, I replied. *But whatever's happening now, it isn't the end. When we mate, it will be on Earth. Not in the Beyond.*

This bright light was uncomfortable, but it wasn't going to kill us. If Jacen wanted to kill us, he had plenty of chances before now. It wouldn't make sense for him to go through all this trouble when he and all of those guards in the throne room could have attacked us the moment we'd teleported into the palace.

Unless he was working with the demons. Which I strongly believed wasn't the case. From what Noah had told me, Jacen and the Earth Angel had been instrumental in fighting against the demons in the Battle at the Vale. Jacen was on our side.

If he weren't, Jessica would have been able to tell that he'd been lying to us this entire time. And I was certain *she'd* never work with the demons.

There was a loud popping sound from where Jacen stood. Then the heat died down until my skin no longer felt like it was burning.

"What the hell was that?" Bella shrieked. "You could have—" She stopped speaking mid-sentence, like something had shocked her to silence.

"I could have what?" Jacen sounded amused.

"Warned us." Her voice was light and airy, like she was in complete disbelief.

"I did," he said. "Not my fault that you didn't listen. And it's safe now, by the way. You all can have a look."

Noah's arms loosened around me, and I opened my eyes, turning around.

The moment I did, I understood why Bella was so dazed.

The cave wall behind Jacen had transformed completely.

It wasn't normal rock, and it wasn't that bright yellow light.

It was a swirling purple vortex. It glowed against an empty black background, like the Milky Way galaxy in space.

"What's that?" I asked, staring at it in awe.

"It's a portal," Bella answered before Jacen had a chance. "But portals don't exist. Not even the most powerful witches have been able to create one."

"Because portals can't be created by a witch," Jacen said simply.

"Did *you* create it?" I asked. "Is that what you were doing with that bright yellow light?"

"The bright yellow light was a security measure," he said. "We can't just let anyone have access to the portal.

It remains hidden down here, only becoming visible to ambassadors of Avalon. The light was angelic magic making sure I was one of those ambassadors."

"So the portal was created by an angel," I said.

"I've told you all I can at this point," Jacen said, although I couldn't help noticing that he didn't say I was wrong, either. "Now, are you ready to step through the portal and begin your journey to Avalon?"

RAVEN

"Yes." I stepped up to the portal, my hand still in Noah's. He stepped up with me, staying right by my side. "We're ready." I spoke for both of us, feeling through the imprint bond that he was as ready as I was.

"You want to go first." Jacen looked at me in admiration. "You're braver than I realized."

"More like impatient to get to Avalon," I said. "But sure. I'll take brave."

"I'd intended on going first to prove it was safe," he said. "But if you want to go first, be my guest. Just know that only one person can go through the portal at a time."

I frowned and tightened my grip around Noah's hand. I'd wanted us to go through together. The thought of going through that swirling purple portal first—and alone—made me feel dizzy and nervous.

And now everyone was watching me, waiting to see how I'd respond.

"Is this part of the Angel Trials?" I asked. "Are you testing us to see if we're brave enough to step through the portal alone?"

Jacen tilted his head slightly and studied me, like he was trying to figure out how to read me. "The Angel Trials aren't something to enter into lightly," he said. "We wouldn't disrespect you by starting the Trials without your consent. When they begin, you'll know. But to start the Trials, you need to be on Avalon. And the only way for you to get to Avalon is through this portal. Like I said, I'm happy to go first. It's perfectly understandable to be wary or scared right now."

I stood straighter when he said the final word. Because I was nervous, yes. But I definitely wasn't *scared*.

I'd been scared a lot lately—when a demon had tried to abduct me in the alley, when I'd come home to find my mom missing, when I had to use Noah's slicer to slay that demon and almost killed myself in the process, when Azazel had kidnapped me and thrown me into that bunker… the list went on.

This was nothing in comparison to all that.

"I've been trying to get to Avalon for weeks," I said. "I'm not scared. I'm *ready*."

"Then by all means…" Jacen motioned ahead. "Lead the way."

I took a deep breath and stared at the swirling portal. Sparks shot out of the ends of it, like stars beckoning me to come through.

You've got this, Noah said through the imprint bond. *I'll be right behind you.*

I know you will. I looked at him, surprised by how proud he looked. Like he was proud of *me*.

We'd come a long way since the beginning of the hunt, when I was a human thorn in his side that he wanted to get rid of and he was an arrogant jerk I couldn't stand.

I'll see you on the other side, I said through the bond.

Then I let go of his hand, stepped up to the swirling portal, and walked through.

RAVEN

I was falling.

Down and down and down, tumbling head over feet, clueless about which way was up. The bright purple of the portal surrounded me like a tube, electrical energy jolts and stars flying by me too fast for me to focus on any of them. I half expected myself to collide with the walls of the portal, but I fell straight down, into a never-ending abyss.

I was supposed to be brave. But I couldn't help it—I screamed.

What else was I going to do when I was tumbling through a portal into what felt like my impending death?

Logically, I knew I wasn't going to die. But my basic

human instincts didn't believe me. Because when someone landed after a fall like this, they died.

Boom. Splat. Dead.

After what felt like the most terrifying minute of my life, I slowed until I was suspended in midair. It felt like floating in water, except I wasn't wet.

There was an ear-splitting crack and a flash of lightning. Then I was slung forward, landing with my hands and knees buried in sand.

I took a few seconds to get my bearings. I was on a beach. I stared straight ahead, where water lapped the ocean shore.

Well, I assumed it was an ocean, but I couldn't tell. Because it was covered in fog so thick that I couldn't see more than a foot past the shoreline.

I'd seen some pretty bad fog in LA, but never anything as dense as this.

I stood up, doing my best to wipe the sand off my hands and knees. I hated sand. It was grainy, gross, and it got stuck on everything. I rarely went to the beach, even though it was right outside my doorstep. I preferred to look at the ocean from the window. Or better yet, from the rooftop patio.

I'd nearly gotten all the sand off of me when a chilly breeze swept though the air. I wrapped my arms around myself, rubbing away the goosebumps that had formed on my skin.

Jacen should have warned us to bring jackets.

At the thought of Jacen, I turned around to see where I'd emerged. There was the portal, right in the side of a towering, rocky cliff.

But the portal was no longer purple. It was blue.

My heart raced, and I looked around in panic. Had I broken the portal when I'd come through it? Was that why it had changed color?

Had I lost the others forever?

Maybe I should try going back through to rejoin up with them. Or would trying to travel through a discolored portal only make things worse?

At the same time, another, quieter voice in the back of my mind told me to relax. I hadn't timed my trip through the portal. But it certainly hadn't been instantaneous.

I needed to give Noah time to come through.

That was the logical thing to do. I took a deep breath and nodded at my decision. I'd wait. If it started to take too long... then I'd worry.

I stared at the portal, not taking my eyes off it for even a second.

Just when the panic was starting to set in again, the portal cracked and flashed a bright, blinding white.

A silhouette that I'd recognize anywhere as Noah's flew out and crashed into me. We both toppled down into the sand.

I landed hard, the breath knocked out of me. At the same time, I was ridiculously relieved. Because Noah was here. The portal wasn't broken.

"Raven!" He sat up and kneeled over me. "Are you okay?" His hands traveled along all parts of my body, making sure nothing was broken. My skin heated everywhere he touched.

I was fine apart from a few bruises. But I stared up into his dark, concerned eyes, tempted to keep lying there so he'd continue his full body examination.

I might have done just that, if I wasn't lying in the sand. And if the next person in our group wasn't going to fly through the portal at any moment.

At the thought of the portal, I glanced at it. It had returned to purple once Noah had come through. Now it was back to blue.

"I'm fine." I sat up and wiped the sand from my arms. He stood and helped me up, and I continued trying to wipe myself free of the sand. But it was hopeless—it was everywhere. Even in my hair. "Ugh. I hate sand."

"You live on the beach." He looked at me like I'd lost my mind.

"So?" I gave my hair a final shake, figuring this was

the best it was going to get. "Doesn't mean I have to like the sand."

"I guess." He shrugged and reached for my arm. "But we should probably move out of the way so the next person who comes through doesn't crash into us."

"Right." I nodded, moving to the side with him.

"Why didn't you move earlier?" he asked. "You knew I was coming through."

"I actually didn't," I said. "When I turned around to look at the portal, it was blue. Like it is now. I thought I'd broken it or something. I was scared that no one else was going to be able to come through, and that I'd be here all alone." I glanced around, still not sure where "here" was. It looked like the Pacific Northwest. But foggier.

"Right. That." Noah glanced at the swirling portal. "Blue means the portal's in use. Purple means it's open."

"How do you know that?"

"Jacen told us after you went through and it turned blue," he said. "We had to wait for it to turn purple to know you were through and it was my turn to go."

"Great." I crossed my arms and let out an aggravated huff. "You'd think he could have told me that *before* I was dumped into this creepy place and thought I broke the portal and would never be able to find you all again." I paused, realization setting in. "Oh, wait. He probably knew exactly what he was doing. I bet he was testing me to see how brave I am."

"You're brave," Noah said simply. "You don't need a test to prove it."

"Thanks." I smiled up at him. "But let's keep the fact that I freaked out before you got here to ourselves, okay? I don't want Jacen to know."

He smirked, clearly amused. "You got it," he said.

The portal flashed lightning again, and Jacen popped out.

Unlike Noah and me, he didn't crash into the sand on all fours. He was prepared and landed gracefully on two feet.

I was glad he hadn't witnessed my graceless entrance. The last thing I needed was for one of the leaders of Avalon to think I didn't have what it took to complete the Angel Trials.

"I see you both made it through in one piece." Jacen walked over to Noah and me, looking us over. "Don't worry about that landing. It gets easier with practice."

How did he know…?

Oh, right. The sand.

If I looked anything like Noah, there were still patches of it that I'd missed getting off.

I. Hated. Sand.

"We knew we had some time before the next person

came through." I shrugged and leaned in suggestively toward Noah. "Can you blame us for having some fun while we waited?"

Noah made a strange sound in the back of his throat, like he was holding in a laugh.

Was I really *that* not believable?

Apparently so, because Jacen looked amused, too. "Whatever you say," he said.

Awkward silence descended between the three of us. It was thicker than the fog.

"So," I said, desperate to change the subject. "What is this place?"

"Good question," Jacen said. "And one that I'll answer once the others arrive. No need to waste time repeating myself when I can wait and tell you all at once."

RAVEN

One by one, the rest of our group tumbled through the portal and fell into the sand.

Jessica came through after Jacen, followed by Bella, the twins, and Harry. Thomas was last, which was a good call. Because the humans were anxious and jittery. Hopefully knowing that a supernatural had their back had helped take some of the edge off on the other side.

In moments like these, I felt like I had more in common with the supernaturals in our group than the humans.

Kara, Keith, and Harry were so unused to the supernatural world. It showed with every anxious, startled look on their faces, and with how they couldn't stop fidgeting.

I, on the other hand, was starting to feel like this *was* my world.

"Welcome to Sir Gawain's Cove." Jacen gestured around as if we could actually *see* the cove through the thick fog. "Sir Gawain was one of the legendary Knights of the Round Table. He was known for his chivalry, his bravery, his compassion, and most importantly, his wisdom. These are all characteristics that citizens of Avalon are expected to have. Once you leave here and head toward Avalon, the island will decide whether it wants to welcome you or send you back to Earth."

"Back up." I held up a hand and looked around in newfound amazement. "You mean we're not on Earth anymore?"

"Correct," Jacen said. "This cove is an anchor island around Avalon. It's only accessible by portal, and it's a required stop for every newcomer. To reach Avalon from here, you must prove your worthiness."

"How do we do that?" Noah's eyes narrowed, like he wasn't sure whether or not to believe Jacen.

I couldn't blame him. The Earth Angel had already sent Noah on a quest to prove his worthiness. He'd completed it by gathering those ten demon teeth. Of course he was skeptical about having to prove himself *again*.

"Guess." Jacen clasped his hands behind his back, looking at us like he knew we wouldn't guess correctly.

Bella gazed out at the dark, gently lapping waves. "Do we swim?" she asked.

"Or climb?" Thomas glanced up at the cliff. His eyes went wide like a child's, like he was excited by the prospect of scaling it.

I hoped his guess was wrong. Noah and Sage's minimal training definitely hadn't prepared me to scale a cliff. I'd fare better swimming through the ocean.

But still, neither option sounded appealing.

"Wrong," Jacen said. "Both of you."

I let out a breath, glad we wouldn't have to do either of those things.

"I can't believe it's not swimming," Bella said. "Demons hate the water."

Jacen ignored her and focused on the rest of us. "What are your guesses?" he asked.

I didn't have one. I could feel through the imprint bond that Noah didn't, either. And Jessica and the three humans were new to the supernatural world. They were more out of their element and clueless than the rest of us.

I crossed my arms and tapped a foot impatiently. "Obviously none of us know." I was annoyed, and I didn't bother hiding it. "So why not get to the point and tell us?"

He chuckled in amusement. "You're just as feisty as Annika warned me you'd be," he said.

"She knows I'm coming?"

"Of course," he said. "After Mary gave me the heads up about who you were, I popped back over to Avalon to let Annika know you'd be on your way. I didn't want her to be shocked at your arrival."

"Right," I said, since it made sense. "But why are you asking us to guess? Why not just tell us what we have to do so we can get started?" I bounced from foot to foot, ready for whatever the next step would be.

"Because unlike Avalon, this cove is accessible to anyone who finds a portal to get here," he said. "That includes demons. I'm asking because I want to understand what someone's initial thought would be to do from here. So far, this hypothetical demon would have tried swimming and climbing the cliff. Which are good things. Because neither of them would get him to Avalon."

"Even if he did the right thing, wouldn't this hypothetical demon be unable to get to Avalon anyway?" Thomas asked. "You told us yourself that the island will judge us to decide whether it wants to give us entry or not. Assuming you're telling us the truth, that would mean this hypothetical demon would be judged as unworthy and sent back to Earth."

"It would," Jacen said. "But it's always best to be prepared for any possible situation."

"True." Thomas gave Jacen a single nod of agreement.

Silence again. Jacen was obviously waiting for one of us to speak up.

"Maybe the answer isn't right where the portal drops us off," I said the first thing that came into my mind. "That would make it too obvious. Maybe we need to explore."

"Smart," Jacen said, and then he winked at Noah. Like, actually *winked*. "She's a keeper."

"I know." Noah stepped in front of me and gave Jacen his scary wolf stare down.

"Relax," Jacen said with a friendly smile. "I'm not trying to steal your girl. In case you've forgotten, there's a beautiful Earth Angel on Avalon who I'm very much in love with. Not even the most charming woman in the world could tempt me away from Annika. No offense," he added, directing the final part at me.

"None taken." I smiled back. "Especially since I'm pretty much as far from 'charming' as it gets."

"Hey." Noah wrapped his arms around my waist and nuzzled into me. "You're charming to me."

Heat flared in my stomach, and I automatically leaned back into him. Every instinct inside of me wanted to pull him closer and mate with him then and there.

The imprint bond was making my hormones go crazy or something.

"Enough of this sickening love fest." Bella rolled her eyes, flipped her hair over her shoulder, and looked around the cove. "Let's do some exploring and figure out the way to Avalon."

RAVEN

Jacen saved us a lot of time by telling us we were wrong every time we had an incorrect guess. Which was good, because we had a *lot* of wrong guesses. There were tons of caves inside the cliffs. We would have been there all day if we'd explored them all. And Kara's perfect sense of direction wasn't any help, since we didn't know what we were looking for.

"Maybe we're not looking in the right place," I said after what felt like over an hour of wandering around aimlessly. "Maybe we need a different vantage point."

"Does that mean you're ready to scale the cliff?" Excitement flashed in Thomas's eyes as he looked at the cliff and back at me.

"Definitely not." I shivered at the thought. "But I'm

from LA, which means I've dealt with my fair share of fog. It hides everything that's not in your immediate vicinity. And this particular fog is thickest over the water. So if there's something we're missing—something that has to do with the water, perhaps—we wouldn't be able to see it from the beach."

"What are you suggesting?" Jacen asked.

"I'm suggesting we step into the ocean," I said. "Not too deep. We can walk back with our feet in the water to see if we can spot anything new. Demons wouldn't want to do this, since like Bella said, they hate the water. Right?"

"Finally." Jacen glanced up at the sky in relief and held out his arms, like he'd been waiting for someone to say it the entire time. "A good idea."

"So I'm right?" I jumped up, giddy with excitement.

"Would I have said that if you weren't?"

"I guess not." I took off my shoes—white sneakers provided to us by the Haven. Then I rolled up my thin white pants so they were above my knees. Holding the shoes in one hand, I ventured out toward the water.

The others did the same.

The moment a wave came ashore and brushed against my toes, I yelped and jumped backward. It was *freezing*. Like this ocean was in the Arctic Circle or something.

"Cold?" Noah asked, amusement flashing through his eyes.

"Why don't you see for yourself?" I challenged.

He stepped into the next wave and sucked in a deep breath the moment his feet made contact with the water.

I smiled, glad that his being supernatural didn't make him magically immune from the cold. Or, his being a *shifter* didn't make him immune to the cold. Because the three vampires in the group—Jacen, Thomas, and Jessica —didn't seem phased by it at all. They simply marched in until the waves were midway up their shins, like the water was the perfect temperature.

Noah and I glanced at each other. In an instant, we rushed to join the vampires. The water was so cold that it burned. I shrieked like a little girl as I ran.

Hopefully we'd get used to it as we kept walking.

Once I joined the others, I saw that I was right. We could see further out into the ocean now that we'd stepped into the fog.

But the whole group wasn't here. Bella, Harry, Kara, and Keith were still on the shore. At least that's where I assumed they were. The fog was so thick that it was impossible to see the beach.

"Are you guys coming?" I screamed out to where we'd been standing.

"Yep," Harry grunted, he and Bella making their way toward us. Harry was holding Keith up on his back, and Bella was holding Kara.

"The water was too cold for them," Bella explained. "So we improvised."

The twins were smiling happily, their arms and legs wrapped around Harry and Bella. They were carefree and relaxed. But I couldn't help feeling concerned.

If they couldn't handle a bit of cold water, how were they going to handle the Angel Trials?

They were too young for this.

Hopefully there'd be another place for them in Avalon—a place where they could contribute without having to join the Earth Angel's army. Hell, *I* didn't feel ready to join an army. I was only doing it to save my mom, and because Noah was going to Avalon. Otherwise, I probably would have stayed at the Haven and tried to help from there.

We waded through the icy water in silence. Finally, just when I was about to give up hope, something took form in the distance.

Brown blobs on top of the water. Rowboats. They were anchored to the water, which was why we couldn't see them from the shore. There were eight of them in all.

Just like there were eight of us journeying to Avalon for the first time.

Bella smirked, like she understood something we didn't. "We're taking boats to get to Avalon," she said. "Just like King Arthur."

"You mean *the* King Arthur?" I asked. "The one who pulled the sword from the stone and ruled Camelot?"

Bella nodded slowly, like my question was beyond stupid.

"But he's a king of myths," I said. "He's not *real*."

The moment the words were out of my mouth, I realized they kind of *were* stupid. Because I'd learned in the past few weeks that most everything I used to believe were myths were real.

Why not add King Arthur and the Knights of the Round Table to that list?

"King Arthur was real," Jacen confirmed. "And he was more than just an average king. Arthur, Lancelet, Guinevere, the Knights of the Round Table... they were all Nephilim. They lived in Camelot and went on quests to kill demons and protect humanity. They were the last of the *good* Nephilim."

"But aren't all Nephilim good?" I asked.

"No." Bella shook her head vehemently. "The only creatures who are truly either good or evil are angels and demons. The rest of us all have free will... choices about what we'll do and who we'll be. The Nephilim were originally created to protect the Earth from the demons still living on it. But King Arthur and the Knights of the Round Table killed the last of the demons. After that, the Nephilim had no purpose anymore. So the next generation turned their sights on killing other creatures they deemed as threats. Their fellow supernaturals."

"Like... you guys?" I looked at the supernaturals surrounding me—people I'd grown to love and see as friends—and shivered in horror at her implication.

"Yes," she said. "The Nephilim became fanatics. They were convinced that supernaturals were a threat to humanity, and that all supernaturals needed to die for humans to be safe on Earth. There was no reasoning with them. No stopping them. They were determined to hunt us to extinction. Which was why a century ago, supernaturals of all species banded together in the Great War and killed the last of the Nephilim."

"Which is why there are no Nephilim around today to kill the demons that escaped the Hell Gate," Jacen continued. "It's why Annika has to create her army from scratch."

"Wow," I said, baffled by the enormity of it all. It was too much to take in at once. Especially when I was freezing in such cold water. "But what do the rowboats have to do with all of this?"

"King Arthur and his Knights killed the last demons in the Battle of Camlann," Bella continued. "It should have been a day to celebrate. But Arthur was wounded during the battle. The witches tried to save him, but their potions didn't work. He was mortally injured. But while dying, an angel sent Arthur a vision. The angel told him not to have a funeral pyre so his body could join his soul in the Beyond. There was a different plan for the great King. And so, Arthur begged those tending to him to place him in a boat so he could sail to his final resting place. Avalon."

"So we're taking boats to Avalon." I glanced at the rickety rowboats creaking in the waves. I was wary about their ability to take us anywhere, let alone to a mystical island. "Just like King Arthur." Then a crazy thought popped into my mind. "Is Arthur still on Avalon today?" I directed the question to Jacen, since he was the only one of the group who had actually set foot on the island.

"I can't tell you that," Jacen said. "But we've been standing here long enough. As you see, there are eight rowboats—one for each of you. I'll be waiting for you on Avalon when those of you deemed worthy arrive. As for those of you *not* deemed worthy, a guard will be waiting at your arrival spot to escort you back to the Vale."

"What happens to those not deemed worthy?" Harry eyed up Jacen, looking worried. Like he thought he might be turned into vampire food or something.

"There are a few options. None of them anything to worry about," Jacen said calmly. "As volunteers to join the Earth Angel's army, you'll be well taken care of, whether on Avalon, the Vale, or the Haven. Now." He walked to the nearest rowboat and gripped the edge of it. "Who wants to get in first?"

"Me." I waded forward, eager to get on with this. I was also eager to get out of the freezing water.

Noah was right by my side, and he took the boat next to mine. The others followed our lead. Bella and Harry placed the twins into boats before getting into ones of their own.

I situated myself inside. The interior of the boat was bare. From the looks of it, it should have been uncomfortable to sit in. But it wasn't. Because once inside the boat, I felt warm. Safe. The fog no longer felt cold against my skin. Instead, it was like a familiar blanket. Like it was telling me not to worry. That everything was going to be okay.

I felt more relaxed than I had in ages.

"Everyone comfortable?" Jacen asked, looking at the group of us.

I nodded, feeling so calm that I couldn't bring myself to talk.

"Great." Jacen must have done something, because the boats unlocked from their anchors and started drifting away from the shore. "Good luck, and I'll see you on Avalon."

RAVEN

*M*y eyes felt heavy the moment I sailed into the mist. It was like the fog was a sedative, urging me to sleep.

I looked to the side to see if Noah was experiencing the same thing. But the fog was so thick that I couldn't see him.

I couldn't see *any* of the others, or their boats.

I was out in the ocean alone. I had no idea how far out my boat had floated. And with each breath I took, my body felt heavier and heavier. Like my blood was turning to lead.

Was this supposed to be happening? Wouldn't Jacen have warned us if the mist were drugged?

I'd had anesthesia once, when I got my wisdom teeth out in high school. This fog felt kind of like that.

I tried to remain sitting up. But my body moved against my will, sliding down, down, down until I was lying in the center of the boat.

I wanted to scream. I wanted to cry out and ask if the others were there—if they were experiencing the same thing.

But my eyes drooped shut, darkness surrounded me, and I had no choice but to surrender to the tranquilizing mist.

RAVEN

I woke to a warm ray of sunlight shining down upon my face.

The boat was no longer beneath me. I was lying on the ground.

How had I gotten from the boat to wherever I was now?

I blinked a few times and sat up, using my hand to guard my eyes from the bright sunlight. I looked around, quickly realizing I was in a giant cavern. There were stalactites and stalagmites everywhere. There was only one break in the ceiling, and that was where the sunlight streaked through.

Panic lodged in my throat. Because I didn't think this was Avalon. Avalon was supposed to be an island, and Jacen had said he was going to meet us there.

Had I been denied entrance to Avalon? Had I been dumped into the "other place" where Jacen said a supernatural guard of the Vale would be meeting me?

Had I failed before I'd even had a chance to begin?

Despair filled my soul, and tears welled in my eyes. My mom was depending on me to get to Avalon and pass the Angel Trials. If I couldn't get to Avalon, how was I going to save her?

She needed me. Yet here I was. Trapped somewhere that clearly *wasn't* Avalon.

Turn around, a deep, male voice echoed in my mind.

I startled and looked around the cave. No one was there.

Where was the voice coming from? It didn't sound like it was coming from anywhere in particular. But I did as it said and turned. I expected to find the person speaking to me behind me.

Instead, I saw four stone pedestals. Each pedestal was about waist height. Upon each of them was a weapon.

A sword. A bow with arrows. A trident. A whip.

Each weapon was shiny, new, and glorious. Like it had been made for royalty.

Touch each weapon to learn about it, the voice spoke again. It echoed not just through my mind, but through the entire cave. Like it was speaking to me from the heavens. *Then choose.*

I looked around the cavern again, searching for the speaker of the voice.

No one was there.

Okay. This was weird. Hearing voices was *not* normal.

What are you waiting for, Raven? The voice spoke again. *Touch each weapon and choose.*

"I was supposed to be going to Avalon." I rotated around as I spoke, wanting to make sure whoever was speaking to me heard. "Where am I? How did I get here?"

You're still on your way to Avalon. Was it just me, or did the voice sound... amused? *If you want a chance at getting there, you need to trust me and follow my instructions.*

"Who are you?" I spoke faster now, panicking. My heart pounded in my throat. I was alone, and scared. I wished Noah were here. "Why should I trust you?"

I'm afraid I cannot answer either of those questions, though you're smart to ask them. The voice sounded sad now, like he desperately wanted me to listen and do as he asked. *All I can do is ask you to look deep into your heart. If following my instructions feels right to you, go ahead and choose a weapon. If not, your journey will end here.*

I swallowed. The voice was being cryptic, but my journey ending here didn't sound good.

You have five minutes, he continued. *Choose.*

Suddenly, large bright yellow numbers appeared on the wall behind the four weapons. Five minutes, counting down by the second.

I didn't like this. I hated being forced to make decisions without being able to ask all the questions I wanted. I especially hated being timed.

But as I stared at the seconds ticking down, an instinctive feeling rushed through me, telling me to do as the voice instructed. Because despite not being able to see who was speaking to me, his voice sounded kind. Trustworthy. Fatherly.

If I didn't do as he'd asked, I'd always look back at this moment with regret. I don't know how I knew it. I just did.

"All right," I muttered, more to myself than to anyone else, and stepped up to the pedestals. "Here goes nothing."

RAVEN

I approached the sword first. I stared at it for a second, unsure what would happen when I touched it.

But the bright numbers ticking down ahead reminded me that time was of the essence. So I reached forward and rested my fingers upon the handle.

The moment I made contact with it, I was no longer in the cave. I was in a beautiful valley. It smelled like spring. There was bright green grass everywhere, a forest up ahead, and chirping animals.

This place was paradise. Too perfect to be real.

And there I was, standing in the middle of it all, wielding the sword. It was as light as ever. I gave it a few practice swings through the air, and red magic danced like flames around the blade. Adrenaline rushed through my veins as I played with the weapon, sensing the power of the magic. It was like I'd been born to hold it.

I was still swinging it around, watching the red magic dancing around the blade, when a large log appeared in front of me. It literally appeared, straight out of thin air. It was being propped up on both ends so it was about two feet above the ground. And somehow, I knew why it was there.

It was there so I could use the sword.

I raised the sword above my head and brought it down on the center of the log. The red magic flared around the sword as it easily sliced through the wood. The log gave no resistance at all. It was like slicing through butter.

Both ends of the log now touched the ground. A perfect, clean cut. Incredible.

The log disappeared, and a sword appeared in its place. It was similar in appearance to mine, but without the magical red glow around it. The blade looked like typical steel. Like the log, it was propped up above the ground.

My magical sword sliced through the normal sword as easily as it had sliced through the log. A clean, perfect cut, again.

The broken pieces of the severed sword disappeared, and a long slab of marble appeared in its place.

My magical sword sliced through that as well. Just as cleanly and easily as everything else.

It shouldn't have been possible. But staring at the incredible sword in my grip, I suddenly understood what it could do.

It had the power to cut through any material, no matter how resistant it would otherwise be to a normal blade.

The moment the thought passed through my mind, the valley disappeared. I was back in the cave, standing over the pedestals. It was like I'd never been in the valley at all—like it had all happened in my mind. And my hand still rested upon the hilt of the sword.

I didn't want to pull away. The sword felt so *right* under my fingers, like it was always meant to be mine. A large part of me wanted to lift it from the pedestal and choose it on instinct.

But I still had four minutes left, and three other magical weapons to learn about. Yes, the sword was alluring. It spoke to me in a way I couldn't explain. It pulsed under my fingers, like it was tied to the beat of my heart.

But what if I felt the same way after touching one of

the other objects? What if one of them called to me even more?

I needed to be smart about my choice.

So I pulled my fingers away from the sword, forcing myself to move onto the weapon on the next pedestal. The bow and arrows.

I reached for the bow and rested my fingers upon it.

RAVEN

*a*gain, I saw myself in the valley, wielding the weapon. An arrow was strung through the bow, the tip of it blazing green with magic.

Ahead of me was a target. Despite having never used a bow in my life, I pulled back my arm, released the arrow, and sent it straight into the bulls-eye.

The target moved farther and farther away. Each time it moved, I shot another arrow at it. Once the arrow landed, the target zoomed forward and presented itself to me.

I hit the bulls-eye every time.

Eventually, the target was so far away that it was beyond my line of sight altogether. Still, I pulled back on the bowstring and shot the arrow in the general area where it must have been.

Bulls-eye. Again.

The bow had the power to always hit its target, no matter how far away the target might be.

Once the realization hit me, I was drawn out of my mind, back to the cave where my fingers laid upon the weapon.

I stared down at it, remembering what it felt like to shoot those arrows. So light and free. The bow was powerful, yes.

But it didn't call to me like the sword.

A glance at the countdown showed only thirty seconds had passed. So I raised my fingers from the bow and moved onto the next item.

The trident.

I placed my fingers upon the gold metal and was in the valley again. I expected to use the trident offensively again—perhaps to throw it and have it land wherever I wanted. But no.

I lifted the trident up so the fork of it was high above my head. It glowed an unearthly blue, and wind whipped around me. The wind grew in strength until some of the smaller trees in the valley were uprooted and blew away.

I wasn't sure how I was still standing strong. I could only attribute it to magic.

After the wind came the lightning. Dozens of strikes,

each one hitting a tree up ahead. Each tree that was hit split down the center, charred and ruined.

I was controlling the weather with the trident. I stared at the ruined trees in front of me—trees that had once been alive and thriving. They were destroyed. Dead.

The once beautiful valley looked like it had been through a hurricane. The grass was drowned, trampled upon, and brown. The chirping animal noises were gone. Silent. Dead. The storm had killed them all.

Destroying such a peaceful place felt wrong all the way down to my bones. It felt *evil*.

I stared at my hand wrapped around the base of the trident, and terror shot through my body at the immense power behind the weapon. It was capable of a level of destruction that scared me. I didn't want to wield such a weapon, no matter how much power came with it.

I dropped the trident down to my feet, not wanting to touch it anymore.

The moment I did, the ruined valley disappeared. I was back inside the cave. My fingers no longer rested upon the terrifying weapon. It sat upon its pedestal, looking no more dangerous than the other weapons.

I knew one thing for sure. I certainly wasn't choosing the trident.

I glanced at the ticking clock—only two minutes left. I'd stayed in the "land of the trident" for longer than all the other weapons.

Quickly, I moved onto the final weapon. The whip. It was made of plain, course rope, as long as a snake. The only part of it that looked magical was the golden handle.

The moment I touched it, I was back in the valley. Thankfully, the valley was no longer destroyed from the trident. It was back to its natural state—trees straight and strong, and animals chirping in the spring breeze. I let out a breath of relief that I hadn't permanently destroyed this beautiful place.

I held the whip awkwardly by my side, unsure what to do. With all the other objects, my mission had been clear.

Maybe I needed to make the first move this time?

I tried twirling the whip around my head and cracking it cowgirl style. It didn't make a sound. So much for that.

Suddenly, something came flying at me from the trees. A stone. It was like someone had catapulted it toward me... except there was no one else in the valley.

I wanted to run out of its path. But my feet were glued to the ground. So I raised my arm and twirled the whip above my head. Unlike last time, the whip shined a glowing yellow. The magic radiated from the weapon, into my hand, and through my entire body.

The whip snapped at the stone and turned it to dust.

I smiled down at the weapon in my hand, amazed I'd pulled off such a feat.

But I didn't have time to pause for long before multiple arrows shot toward me. They came from the same place in the trees as the stone, appearing from what looked like nothing.

The whip took on a mind of its own, twirling and cracking around the arrows, turning each one to dust before it could hit me. With the weapons in my hand, I moved with startling speed, like a cobra. It was like the whip and I shared a mind of our own.

The moment the arrows stopping coming at me, the bright yellow magic faded from around the whip. It was back to normal.

I waited a bit for something else to fly at me. Nothing happened. The attacks seemed to be over.

Curious, I walked toward a small tree nearby, twirled the whip, and tried to wrap it around the trunk.

I missed by a foot.

The whip must have the power to stop anything from harming its owner. It was a defensive weapon— not an offensive one. Completely the opposite of the trident. The magic would only help me if I were being attacked.

The moment I realized the nature of the whip's power, the valley disappeared around me and I was back in the cavern. My fingers were laid upon the beautiful golden handle of the weapon.

I glanced at the countdown on the wall. Fifteen seconds.

How had so much time passed while I was in the valley with the whip?

I didn't have time to contemplate it. Because if I didn't make a choice before the timer hit zero, this was over.

I still wasn't sure what "this" was, but I didn't want it to be over. So I needed to choose a weapon. Now.

Three seconds. It looked like I was relaying on gut instinct here.

I walked over to the one that called to me the most, lifted it from the pedestal, and raised it above my head. "This," I declared to the mysterious, all-knowing voice, "is the weapon I choose."

RAVEN

*T*he countdown stopped with one second to go. All of the other pedestals—and the weapons upon them—vanished.

A bold choice, the voice said.

I swallowed, unsure if that was a good thing or not.

Four powerful weapons were presented before you, the voice continued. *Why did you choose the sword?*

He asked it like I had a long time to make my decision, instead of merely seconds.

"It called to me." I shrugged. "When I used the sword it felt *right*."

And when you used the other weapons?

I turned around to look behind me. Hopefully the man behind the voice might present himself now that I'd made my decision.

No one was there.

I was still speaking to a magical, disembodied voice in the cave. Whoever this guy was, he really wanted to remain impersonal.

"The trident felt awful," I started with the most obvious one. "There was something dark about it. Something evil. Something I didn't want to claim as mine." I shivered just thinking about the ruined valley the trident had left in its wake. "Both the bow and the whip felt good to use, but neither of them felt right for me."

Can you elaborate?

I pressed my lips together and studied the sword in my hand, thinking about how to explain why the sword was right and the others were wrong. "The bow needs to be used at far range, which would put me at risk in close up combat," I said. "And the whip can only be used defensively, not offensively. I felt like it controlled me instead of the other way around. So I guess I chose the sword because it gives me the most control."

The voice didn't reply. The silence felt like a physical thing in the air pressing down upon me.

I tightened my grip around the handle of the sword, worried I'd said something wrong. To a voice that was talking to me from either thin air or inside my mind.

Maybe all this supernatural stuff had driven me crazy once and for all.

You guess? he finally asked.

"No." I swallowed and stood straighter. "It's not a guess. This sword is a powerful weapon, and I chose the because it gives me the most control."

With that, the cave wall before me cracked in two. Light shined out from the crack, like it was beaming inward from the Heavens. The walls moved outward like sliding doors, revealing a red clay path winding around a grassy hill. I knew it was red clay from my brief time playing tennis. Some of the courts I'd played on had been made of the same material.

Thank you, Raven, the voice said. *You've chosen well. Continue to follow the path and make any decisions necessary along the way. Good luck, and I'll see you soon.*

A warm breeze blew through the cave. I had a feeling that the voice—whoever he was—was gone.

"Seriously?" I looked up at the ceiling in annoyance. "That's it? You're giving me a magical sword, telling me to be off on my way, and not telling me where I am or *why* any of this is happening at all?"

No answer.

I huffed and threw down my arm. The tip of the sword met the ground with so much force that I was nearly thrown off balance.

I wasn't supposed to be here. I was supposed to be in Avalon.

Unless… maybe this place *was* Avalon?

There was only one way to find out.

And so, sword in hand, I headed out of the cave, ready to see what waited for me outside.

RAVEN

*O*nce I stepped out of the cave, a belt appeared around my waist with a sheath for the sword.

"Cool," I said, sliding the sword into place. It clicked into position, and then was weightless. For a moment I worried it had disappeared entirely. But I pulled it out, and it was completely in tact.

This sword had all kinds of nifty tricks up its sleeve.

Placing the sword back inside the sheath, I walked along the clay path leading out of the cave. The sun shined brightly up ahead. It was a beautiful spring day, with birds chirping and the smell of flowers in the air. It was practically calling for me to hang out and bask in the perfect weather.

But I didn't have time to stop and enjoy the scenery. I needed to continue on.

The cave had been inside a big hill, and the path led out and over it. So off I went. I crossed my fingers that once I came over the crest, I'd find Noah, Jacen, and the others waiting for me.

I didn't.

All I saw were more and more grassy, green hills rolling out toward the horizon. It was the same way every direction I turned. Rolling hills, as far as the eye could see. It was like I'd been plopped right in the middle of nowhere in New Zealand. Except there were no sheep.

The path I was on also continued out toward the horizon. How far was I expected to walk?

The guy who'd told me to follow it must really want me to work on my cardio.

But what other choice did I have? So I took a deep breath and trudged forward. I kept going and going and going.

I wasn't wearing a watch, so I had no idea how long I'd been walking. Hours, probably. All I knew was it was long enough that I'd worked up a good sweat and had blisters on my feet. It was also long enough for the weather to change. Clouds had rolled into the previously clear skies.

Hopefully it wouldn't start raining. Although, maybe

rain would be a good thing. All of this walking was making me thirsty.

Just when I was starting to feel dizzy from the thirst, the path led me to a burbling stream. It was like a fairy stream, with big mossy stones surrounding it. A line of stones led across the water to where the path continued on the other side.

I sank down onto a large stone next to the bank, cupped my hands together to gather the water, and drank. I gulped down as much water as possible, not knowing when I'd get this chance again.

Hopefully the water was safe. But the stream was moving fast and the water didn't look dirty, so it seemed fine.

After drinking so much water that my stomach felt like it might burst, I lowered my hands and looked up.

I startled at what I saw and fell back onto my butt —hard.

Because two animals stood on the other side of the stream, watching me curiously. And they weren't just *any* old animals.

They were a unicorn and a dragon.

The unicorn was pure white, with a gleaming silver horn coming out of its forehead. It stood tall, proud, and majestic, its white mane and tail blowing in the wind.

The dragon was all black except for its glowing yellow eyes. Its arms were melded into its wings like a pterodactyl. It would have been terrifying if it weren't perched peacefully on its legs with its head tilted to the side, watching me expectantly.

Once I'd gotten a good look at both of the creatures, the clouds in the sky above them formed into shapes.

No, not shapes. Numbers. *Moving* numbers.

A forty-second countdown.

I knew what that meant. Choose.

And given the short amount of time on the clock, I wasn't getting a chance to learn about either of the creatures this time. I was going to have to go with my gut.

Luckily, this choice was easy.

I hopped over the stones to cross the stream and ran up to face the two creatures. I couldn't believe they were real. But here they were, right in front of me, staring down at me and waiting expectantly.

Thirty seconds.

I needed to be quick. But these were living beings. I didn't know how much they understood what was going on, and I wanted to be kind about my choice.

"You both are beautiful," I said, looking back and forth between the two of them as I spoke. "I wish I could choose both of you to come along with me to… well, to wherever we're going. But I can't." I turned to the dragon now, putting as much apology into my tone as possible. "Unfortunately, I'm not very good with heights. And while I've never flown on anything, I've had experience horseback riding in the past." I bit my lip after saying that bit and glanced at the unicorn, hoping I hadn't accidentally insulted it.

I must have, because the unicorn hoofed at the ground with its front leg and gave me what I could only describe as an irritated side eye.

"Not that a horse is anywhere near as magnificent as you are, of course," I said, as if such a thing would be ridiculous. "But I feel like the experience will be beneficial."

That must have placated the unicorn, because it stilled once more and lifted its neck proudly. Its mane shimmered as it blew in the wind.

I could have stood there admiring both creatures for hours. But a glance up at the sky showed I had fifteen seconds left.

I needed to hurry up.

I also needed to make sure I didn't accidentally turn either creature into an enemy. They were both acting peacefully now, but I had a feeling that both of them had the potential to be very, very dangerous.

So I turned once more to the dragon. I couldn't be sure, but I could have sworn its lips were curved up into a small smile. "I hope to meet you again in the future, when I'm better prepared for flight," I finished up. "Then it'll be your turn. But right now, I choose the unicorn."

I stepped up to the unicorn and placed my hand on its warm neck, sealing my choice.

RAVEN

Three things happened when I placed my hand on the unicorn and declared my choice.

The countdown cleared from the sky.

The dragon raised its wings and took off. It flew away until it was a mere dot on the horizon, and then, until it disappeared completely.

My mind was flooded with information about the unicorn.

She was female, and her name was Annar. She was two hundred and thirteen years old. She had a mate and a child back home. Her favorite food was watermelon.

And she was happy I'd chosen her.

"I'm happy I chose you, too," I said as I ran my

fingers lovingly along her neck. Her fur was softer than the finest silk.

It was a good thing humans didn't know about the existence of unicorns. I shuddered to think of what they'd do with fur as soft as this.

As I stroked her, I wondered how I was supposed to get on her. The horses I'd ridden back in summer camp had always been saddled. But from the tall, proud way Annar stood, I had a distinct impression that unicorns weren't the type of creature that liked to be saddled.

Apparently I'd have to wing this.

I also didn't want her first impression of me to be my trying to jump onto her back, missing, and somehow falling with my face next to her hoof. Because knowing me, that was something that might happen.

"I guess you can't kneel down so I can get onto your back, can you?" I asked lightly.

She dug her hoof into the ground, let out a small huff, and stood taller.

Well, there was the answer to that question.

So I looked around. My gaze instantly landed on the big rocks along the stream. Some of them were definitely tall enough to give me the step up I needed.

I walked over to one of the larger rocks—it went up to about my knee—and stepped up onto it. "Annar?" I said her name tentatively. I didn't want to give the unicorn commands, since she seemed like the stubborn type. We needed to work together. "It'll be easier for me to get on your back from up here."

She held my gaze, her kind black eyes focused on mine. Then she headed over to where I was standing on the rock. Once she reached me, she rotated so I could get on her back.

She was still tall, even given my additional height. But with what little physical strength I had, and with a lot of determination, I managed to pull myself up onto her back. Not as gracefully as I would have liked, but hey, I'd work on that.

Sitting on her bare back was as cozy as sitting on a cloud. It must have been special unicorn magic.

From this view, I could see her horn from much closer. It was large, probably about half the size of my arm. Sunlight glinted off of it, and it sparkled like diamonds. But it wasn't diamonds, because it was silver. It took my breath away. Clearly it was some kind of magical, otherworldly material that wasn't from Earth.

Again, I was relieved that unicorns hid themselves from humans. Given what humans did for elephant tusks, I'd hate to know what they'd do for the unearthly material in a unicorn horn.

Annar nodded her head, as if agreeing with my thought.

"So," I said, looking forward along the path. "My instructions in the cave were to continue along the red clay path. It's been a pretty long journey so far, and I don't see an end in sight. Would you like to help me get there faster?"

I was careful to phrase my request as a question and not a command.

Annar flipped her mane up and over her shoulder, so the hair rested near my hands. Then an image formed in my mind.

It was of myself sitting on top of her back, my hands fisted tightly around the hair of her mane.

She must have put the image into my mind somehow. She was telling me to use her hair to hold on.

I did as instructed, twining her gleaming white hair tightly through my fingers. The moment I did, my body hummed with magic, from my hands all the way down to my toes. It was like a tether formed between us, connecting me to Annar. I felt solid on her back. Like no matter what crazy moves she made, I wasn't going anywhere.

She shot forward in a full out gallop. My stomach lurched, like at the start of a roller coaster. It was a miracle I hadn't fallen off her back.

No, it wasn't a miracle. It was unicorn magic.

Wind rushed past my face, the hills whizzing by.

Annar was galloping faster than a car on a freeway. We must have been going eighty or ninety miles per hour. And once I settled into the speed, it felt *amazing*. The sword sheathed to my waist kept hitting her side, but it didn't seem to bother her. I felt through the bond that she was enjoying running as much as I was.

After about thirty minutes, something peeked into view along the horizon. Tree tops.

The hills were ending, and we were approaching the beginning of a forest.

Would Annar be able to run as quickly in the forest? Or would the trees get in the way?

I was contemplating it as she ran around the corner of the final hill and came to a jolting stop. If I hadn't been on a unicorn, I would have gotten whiplash. As it was, I was just startled.

I looked up, curious about what had caused her to stop so suddenly.

And the moment I saw what was blocking our path, I froze in fear.

RAVEN

*B*locking the path straight ahead of us was a monster that looked to be a cross between Big Foot and Chewbacca.

He was a giant, ape-like creature, naked minus a loincloth tied around his waist. He was half the size of a tree... and chained to one by one of his wrists. He tugged and tugged at the chain, but no matter how hard he tugged, the tree didn't budge.

It must have been a strong chain. *Magically* strong.

At the sight of us, he let out a roar so loud it vibrated in my chest. He tried running toward us, but the chain pulled tight and stopped him in his tracks. He bared his teeth and let out another angry wail.

Annar stood firm in the ground. From where we were outside the radius of the chain, the monster couldn't reach us. But we couldn't continue on the path with the monster there, either.

"Maybe we can go around him?" I asked once he'd finished screaming. "We can find another way into the forest and rejoin the path there. He can't hurt us if we don't get within the radius of his chain. Right?"

Annar remained where she was standing. Unbelievable. I thought my suggestion was perfectly logical. Yet she was acting like I hadn't spoken at all.

I tried using my feet to nudge her to the side. But she held her head higher, ignoring me.

Wow. This unicorn was more stubborn than I was.

I looked off to both sides, trying to see if there was another entrance to the forest. There wasn't. The trees were so thick it would be impossible for Annar to walk through them without getting tangled in their branches.

What other options did I have? I certainly didn't plan on jumping off Annar and going into the forest alone. We were a team now—we were getting to the end of this path together. Plus, I didn't want to leave her alone with this monster. She'd probably just turn around and go back to wherever she'd come from. But leaving her here alone didn't feel right.

That only left me with one choice. If we couldn't go around the monster, we'd have to go through it.

This was normally the point where I'd sit back and

let Noah and Sage do the dirty work. But they weren't here right now. And I had the perfect weapon to get us out of this mess.

I reached for the handle of the sword and pulled it out of its sheath. The sound of the metal coming out of its casing sounded downright melodic. I held the sword in front of me with both hands, red magic dancing around the blade as it came to life.

It was now or never. Surely it wouldn't be easy to fight this monster, since he was many times the size of me. But this sword could cut through anything. All I needed was the right angle to get in a clean sweep that would slice him neatly in two.

I could do this. I *needed* to do this, so I could continue along this path and hopefully find Noah and the others again.

And so, I eyed up the monster before me and took a deep breath, readying myself to ask Annar to run forward so I could attack.

Before I could, the monster looked out to the hills, threw his free arm back, and let out a long, agonized wail.

His cry was so loud that the treetops rustled. And it sounded like he was in pain. Not physical pain, although I imagined it couldn't be comfortable to have your wrist chained to a tree. His cry was that of *emotional* pain. Deep, emotional pain that shook me down to the core.

His wail finally stopped when he ran out of breath.

I studied him over the tip of my sword. "Why are you chained to this tree?" I asked. "Who put you here?"

He watched me with sad eyes and let out another long, sad cry. I didn't know if he understood me. But he clearly couldn't answer back.

I lowered my sword, not wanting to appear like a threat. Because I knew eyes like his. I'd seen them when I'd been locked in the bunker with the other gifted humans.

They were the eyes of someone who was trapped, scared, and helpless.

It was easy to assume this creature was dangerous because of his size. And upon first encounter, his loud screams were frightening.

But looking into his eyes, I believed they were the cries of a creature chained up for something he couldn't control—what he'd been born as. Not as someone who wanted to attack.

There was only one right thing to do here.

I placed my free hand upon Annar's neck, sending my plans to her through the bond. "What do you think?" I asked her. "Will you help?"

She nodded her assent.

Next, I raised my hand in the air, trying to communicate with the giant. He watched me like I'd lost my marbles. So, trying again, I pointed to him and raised my hand once more.

He raised his free hand in return and shook it manically.

I shook my head and pointed toward his other hand. The hand bound to the tree.

He frowned and gave another tug on the chain. He followed it up with another sad wail, still giving the chain the occasional tug.

The fur under his eyes was wet now. He was crying.

I nodded and raised my hand again. Then, with the hand holding the sword, I slowly swung the open air next to my hand. Then I pointed back to him.

He wailed and tugged on the chain again. He shook his head in a "no" motion, more tears wetting the fur under his eyes.

I had no idea if this was going well or not. It didn't seem like it was. But the chain was pulled taut right now. This was my chance.

"Now, Annar." I used my free hand to hold onto her hair, and she ran forward.

When we reached chain, I swung my sword down at it, slicing it cleanly in half.

I pulled back on Annar's hair, using it like a rein. A

second later I realized that might irritate her, but she obeyed my request to halt, and turned us to face the giant.

He raised his now free arm in the air and stared at us in amazement. He looked to the tree, the broken chain, and us again. Finally, he cheered and jumped three times. With each jump, the ground shook, and I held tighter onto Annar's mane to stay in place.

Once he finished his celebration, he walked toward us and held out his hand that had been chained. There was still a shackle around his wrist. A piece of the chain hung from it. He pointed to the shackle and then at my sword, tilting his head in question.

He wanted me to remove it. But it was bound so tightly around his wrist. I feared that if I tried removing it, I'd end up hurting him in the process.

I looked up into his eager eyes, dreading having to shake my head and tell him that no, I couldn't remove the shackle.

But before I could, Annar rotated around so she faced him. She lowered her head and touched the tip of her gleaming horn to the shackle.

The shackle shimmered and disappeared into thin air. The chain that had been bound to it dropped to the ground at our feet.

The giant's wrist was chafed and bloody from who

knows how long being shackled to that tree. But he was free.

He reached into a pocket in his loincloth and pulled out two golden apples. They were the size of normal apples, but looked tiny in his oversized hand. They also truly were golden, with a metallic, shimmering skin.

Surely they weren't edible?

He lowered the first one toward Annar's mouth. The unicorn chomped down on the fruit, consuming it in a few bites.

Now the giant looked expectantly at me, holding the apple out toward my face.

I plucked it from his hand, studying it and examining its strange metallic sheen. Normally I would have been afraid to eat it. But Annar had eaten it with no hesitation. Nothing bad had happened to her. Plus, I was really hungry. And the giant was still watching me, waiting. I had a feeling he wouldn't take it well if I refused.

So here went nothing.

I opened my mouth wide and took a large bite out of the shiny apple.

It. Was. Amazing.

Not just the taste. Because yes, the juice was like liquid sunshine, and the fruit was perfect and sweet. But this apple must have been magical. Because as I ate it, my hunger and thirst subsided into nothing. And most amazingly, my energy shot up like crazy.

I'd been living in such a state of anxiety and exhaustion these past few weeks that I'd gotten used to it. But after eating the apple, I felt fresh, energized, and ready to take over the world. I hadn't felt so awake and clear headed ever, to be honest. And amazingly, every bit of the apple was edible, including the core.

"Thank you," I said to the giant, using the back of my hand to wipe any excess juice off my mouth. "That was delicious."

The giant smiled and nodded, his eyes shining with happiness that I'd enjoyed the apple. I couldn't believe that less than fifteen minutes ago, I'd contemplated using my sword to slice him in half. He was a kind, gentle soul. I was glad I'd seen that before doing something awful.

He smiled again—like he knew what I was thinking —before turning around and running gleefully off into the hilly landscape behind us.

He was free. I hoped wherever he was going, it was to return to others like him.

Which was exactly what I needed to do, too.

And so, Annar and I faced forward, ready to continue along the red clay path that led straight into the dark forest.

RAVEN

I did *not* want to enter that forest.

The trees were so tall that they looked like they went up into the sky forever. It was dark, dense, foggy, creepy, and basically everything a normal person would avoid. Unless they were trying to get themselves killed.

To make things even creepier, the moment we stepped into the forest, it was suddenly nighttime. When we'd freed the giant, the sun was high up in the sky, not anywhere close to setting.

Now it was gone. And the treetops were so thick that when I tried looking up to see the moon, all I saw were branches and leaves. The only bright thing in the entire area was Annar's gleaming horn leading our way. Without her horn, it would have been pitch dark.

Owls hooted up ahead, and I heard other, strange noises coming from animals I didn't dare try to picture. Given everything I'd encountered in this place so far, it was safe to assume I wasn't on Earth anymore. So whatever creatures lurked in these woods... I was probably better off not knowing what they were.

We'd only been walking in the forest for a minute when a giant spider dropped down in front of us. I shrieked and leaned back. The spider was literally four feet wide, and I could see every gross, disgusting detail of its eyes, hairy body, and most disturbingly, its pinchers.

I hated spiders. And judging by the way this one was eyeing us up and moving its pinchers in and out, it was ready to have us for dinner.

But I'd already come this far. I wasn't going to end up a spider's meal.

I needed to gather my wits and handle this.

So I took a deep breath and reached for my sword, ready to do whatever was necessary to continue along the path. Even if that meant facing off with this giant spider.

I signaled to Annar to go forward. But as we got closer, the spider crawled back up into its web, giving us space to continue along the path.

It was like the spider had gotten a whiff of us and decided we wouldn't be a satisfying meal.

I kept my eyes on it the entire time we walked underneath it, ready to use my sword in a second's notice. But it let us pass.

"Huh," I said, placing my sword back into its sheath. "That was easy."

It was *too* easy.

Warmth flowed into my hands through Annar's mane, and she sent another image into my mind. Not an image—a memory. Of both of us eating the golden apples.

But now I saw that when we ate the apples, a sparkly, golden protective aura formed around us. A shield. The shield was still around us as we walked through the forest. I couldn't see it myself, but from the image Annar sent me, the creatures of the forest could. It signaled them not to attack.

"Are you telling me the apples gave us some kind of invincibility shield?" I asked, my mind blown. I used to play the video game Mario Kart as a kid. One of my favorite moments was when I got an invincibility star and was immune to attacks. From what Annar was showing me, the golden apples seemed similar to that star.

Annar nodded, confirming my suspicion.

Wow. I wished I could go back and thank the giant. I'd known the golden apple had made me feel great, but I hadn't known the full extent of its powers.

I shuddered to think about what we might have had to face in this forest without the golden apples protecting us.

Once past the spider, Annar burst back into a gallop. We were out of the forest in thirty minutes tops.

I had a feeling it would have taken a *lot* longer without the protection of the apples.

We stepped out of the forest into a gorgeous purple sunset over more rolling hills. But the path didn't continue in one single lane like it did before.

It forked into four separate paths. All of them made of the same red clay.

At the end of each path were enchanting abodes. They were far away, but close enough that I could still see what they were.

A massive stone castle overlooking a welcoming, magical forest.

A palace by the sea that looked like a golden version of Oz.

A Grecian mansion so high up in a mountain that it was practically part of the clouds.

And lastly, a cozy Victorian house with smoke

coming out of the chimney, surrounded by fertile farmland.

Once I looked at each of houses, another timer appeared in the sunset streaked clouds. Thirty seconds.

Seriously? Whoever was in charge of this strange quest certainly enjoyed forcing me to make gut decisions.

With no time to waste, I looked at each choice again. The Victorian house reminded me *way* too much of the bunker I'd been trapped in with the other gifted humans. So that one was out. I didn't like heights, so no thanks to the mansion in the sky, no matter how beautiful it was. And I'd had enough of forests for one day.

"The palace by the sea," I said, the decision easy. I'd grown up next to the ocean. Of course the palace by the sea called to my heart.

Annar's horn glimmered in what I thought was happiness, and we galloped toward the golden palace.

I had no idea what was waiting for me inside.

Hopefully someone who could give me answers.

Because at this point, I sure had a lot of questions.

*A*nnar and I rode up to the massive double door entrance of the palace. Once she stopped, I took a deep breath of a fresh sea air and looked up at the building in awe.

The golden spires twinkled with light. I felt so small next to it. The towers were so high that they went up into the sky. I couldn't imagine what the inside of this splendid palace must look like.

Suddenly, a step stool appeared beside Annar. It was the perfect height to help me get off her back. I had no idea how it got there. It literally appeared out of thin air.

This place I was in—wherever it was—was weird.

I jumped off the unicorn's back, sadness growing in my heart as I did so. Once on the ground I turned to her and placed a hand lovingly on her neck. "I guess unicorns aren't allowed inside the palace, are they?" I asked.

She shook her head no. There was sadness in her eyes, too.

"So this is where we say goodbye?" The words were hard to say. Despite the short time we'd spent together, I'd grown attached to Annar. It felt like the two of us had been destined to meet.

She nodded yes.

"Will I ever see you again?" I asked.

She touched the tip of her horn to my forehead, and a warm, female voice echoed through my mind. "I hope so," she said.

I blinked once she pulled away, shocked. "You can talk?"

Well, she hadn't really *talked*. But she'd spoken to my mind. Which I definitely hadn't realized she could do.

Her lips curved up into a knowing smile, and she touched her horn to my forehead again. "Of course I can communicate with words," she said, as if anything else would be ridiculous. "I'm simply picky about who I choose to communicate with. And you Raven Danvers, have certainly proven yourself to me. Now, go into that palace and prove yourself to him."

"Who's 'him?'" I looked over my shoulder at the

palace in worry. The beautiful building now seemed more intimidating than ever.

When I turned back at Annar, she was gone. The step I'd used to dismount was gone, too. She'd disappeared into thin air. Like she'd never existed at all.

My heart dropped. "Annar?" I called out for her, although I knew she wouldn't come.

No answer. All I heard was the breeze whistling through palm trees and the waves lapping along the shore.

Tears welled in my eyes at the disappearance of my new friend, and I blinked a few times, letting them roll down my cheeks. "Goodbye." I looked out to the ocean, knowing she couldn't hear me, but hoping she somehow could. "Thank you—for everything. And I hope we see each other again, too."

As I was looking out, a big dark cloud rolled in. Thunder echoed from out in the distance, and I saw droplets falling down into the ocean. Rain.

If that wasn't a sign for me to go inside, I didn't know what was. So I wiped the tears from my cheeks and stepped toward the towering doors. They were so tall—about four times my height. Tall enough for a giant to enter.

Perhaps I'd be reunited with the giant I'd saved from the tree. But he'd run the other direction. And I had a feeling from what Annar had said that the person I'd be meeting at this palace would be powerful. Not just in strength, but in wisdom, too.

The thunder rumbled louder now. The rain was getting closer.

I looked around for a doorbell and found none. So I raised my hand and gave three strong knocks, hoping whoever was inside would be close enough to hear.

I was debating trying to knock again when the doors creaked open, welcoming me inside.

The foyer was as big as a ballroom. There were marble floors, a gorgeous golden chandelier, and a grand staircase that split off into two and curved around the walls. There was even a wooden treasure chest pressed against the far wall.

"Hello?" I stepped inside and looked around, feeling as lost and out of place as Maria in *The Sound of Music* when she walked into the Von Trapp mansion for the first time. "Is anyone home?"

It was dead quiet.

Whoever Annar said was waiting for me inside the palace clearly didn't feel like my arrival was important enough to bother greeting me.

Unless I had to find him. This whole experience was so strange that I wouldn't be surprised if that were the case.

As I was contemplating where to begin, the chest creaked open.

Bright, yellow numbers appeared on the inside of the top. Five minutes. Not surprisingly, the numbers were counting down.

I hurried over to the chest, kneeled down in front of it, and looked inside. There were four vials. Each was filled with a different color liquid. Green, yellow, blue, and red.

Clearly, I had to choose one of them. But I doubted whoever was giving me this test was asking me which one of the four colors was my favorite. There had to be more to it.

The only other time I'd been given five minutes to make a decision in this place had been when I had to choose one of the four weapons. I'd been able to touch those and see their inherent powers.

Maybe I could do the same with these vials of liquid?

I reached for the one on the far left—the green one. The moment I touched it, I *knew* what drinking it would do.

It would give me unlimited wealth.

I don't know how I knew. I just did. Touching it made the knowledge of what the potion could do pop into my mind.

I touched the other three potions, learning what they could do, too.

The yellow one would give me immortality. The blue one would give me endless knowledge. The red one would give me strength greater than any supernatural.

Four minutes left on the clock. And I sensed the four minutes would feel like they passed quickly, because this was a *huge* decision.

I looked around the grand foyer of the palace, searching for clues that *someone* was there. "Who are you?" I asked into the void. "Why are you offering me this?"

No answer. But the numbers on the countdown glowed brighter, as if they were telling me to hurry up and make my choice.

I refocused on the four vials inside the chest.

There was one potion I definitely wouldn't drink right now—the yellow one that would give me immortality. Mainly because the people I loved most in the world weren't immortal. How could I be immortal and watch them all grow old and die? I'd mate with Noah, and he'd grow old while I stayed the same. Then once he passed onto the Beyond, I'd remain on Earth forever. And because of the way mating worked, I'd never find love again.

So yeah, that was a definite pass on the immortality.

Drinking the green potion for wealth was illogical when there was the blue potion for knowledge sitting beside it. With unlimited knowledge, I'd be able to acquire wealth on my own. So it was easy to eliminate the green one.

My eyes flicked between the blue vial for endless knowledge and the red vial for total strength. Two completely opposite things. One for the mind and the other for the body.

After everything I'd been through these past few weeks, I definitely wanted strength. The situations I'd been faced with would have been so much easier if I'd been stronger than a supernatural, instead of the weak human that I was. So the red vial was certainly tempting.

But endless knowledge provided so many possibilities. Ones that went beyond strength and wealth. How many people could be helped if I had the knowledge about how to help them? How many lives could I save?

Plus, endless knowledge would give me knowledge about how to be a better fighter. Sure, I wouldn't have strength that out powered any supernatural. But I'd have the knowledge about how to defeat any enemy I faced.

It was the most useful of all the potions in the long term.

And so, my decision was made.

I reached for the blue vial and lifted it to my lips, getting ready to drink.

But right before the liquid touched my tongue, the vial disappeared into thin air, along with all of the others. The timer stopped counting down, and the top of the chest slammed shut.

"Really?" I couldn't help rolling my eyes. "You aren't going to let me drink it? You just wanted to see which one I'd pick?"

I didn't expect an answer. So I wasn't disappointed when I didn't get one.

But I *was* surprised when golden, glowing arrows appeared on the floor by my feet. They led through the foyer and up the grand staircase.

Directions for where I was heading next.

I followed the glowing arrows up the steps and into the long hall on the second floor. The hall was just as grand as the foyer, with rows and rows of doors inside of it.

Where did all these doors lead? Part of me wanted to open one and look.

But this wasn't my home. I couldn't just go opening doors and disturbing whatever might be behind them. Especially when the arrows clearly had a destination in mind for me.

I had no idea who was leading me on this journey. It

could be the voice I'd heard in the cavern, Annar, or someone else I hadn't met yet. But they hadn't led me off track so far.

I needed to stay the course.

Eventually, the arrows led me to one of the doors on the right side of the hall. This door didn't look any different or more special than the others. But the arrows pointed toward the door and under it. Like they were telling me to enter.

I opened the door and walked into a bedroom. There was an ornate canopy bed in the center of the room... and Noah was lying on it.

RAVEN

There was a man sitting beside the bed, and a cradle next to him. But I didn't care about either of them.

All I cared about was Noah.

I called out his name and ran toward him. His eyes were closed, his skin paler than normal. But the imprint bond pulled me toward him, the connection between us pulsing like a living thing.

"Noah," I repeated his name as I sat down on the bed next to him. I took his hand in mine, but he didn't wake. He didn't even respond when I tried reaching out through the imprint bond.

His body was here, but it was like *he* wasn't here at all. There was something wrong with his soul. It was dim. Unreachable. I didn't want to feel it before, but now that I did, I couldn't believe I'd missed it.

My gaze shot up to the man sitting at his bedside. He looked to be in his thirties, and he was watching me patiently. He hadn't said a word this entire time. He was just watching... like he was waiting.

Creepy.

"Who are you?" I asked, continuing before he could answer. "And what did you do to Noah?"

"I'm Dr. Lake," he answered calmly. "And I can assure you, I didn't do anything to Noah. I'm here to take care of my patients. Both of them." He motioned to Noah and the cradle on his other side.

A baby girl slept in the cradle. She was just as pale and still as Noah. It would have been easy to mistake her as a doll instead of a living creature.

I gripped Noah's hand tighter, hoping this was just a dream. His body heat normally ran hotter than normal. But right now, his hand was so cold.

"This isn't real." I shook my head, not wanting to believe that this—whatever *this* was—was happening. "The last time I saw Noah, we were getting into the rowboats to go to Avalon. He wasn't sick. He shouldn't be like this."

"Since then, he's been cursed," Dr. Lake said. "A witch

cast a deadly dark magic spell on him. He only has a few hours left to live."

"What?" It was too much for me to take in at once. I wasn't used to seeing Noah like this. So weak. So helpless. Everything he wasn't. And we still hadn't mated. We had our entire lives ahead of us. I refused to believe this was the end. "Don't you have a cure?" I asked. "Some way to save him?"

"Yes." The doctor nodded. "I have an antidote pill for the curse."

Relief rushed through my chest. Noah was going to be okay. "How long will it take to kick in?" I asked.

I couldn't wait for Noah to wake up so he could tell me how he'd gotten into this mess with a dark witch in the first place.

Knowing him, it would be a good story.

"I haven't given it to him yet," the doctor said.

"Why not?" I looked up at him in confusion, my entire body tensed in anger. "You said he only has hours left. Give him the antidote pill. Now."

"I'm afraid it's not that easy." The doctor studied me, his expression grim. "You see, there's only one antidote pill in existence. And both Noah and this young girl Selena have been put under the same curse." He motioned to the baby in the cradle—Selena. "A trustworthy prophet has declared that Selena is destined to be a savior to the supernatural community, and the world at large. Her death will have dark consequences."

I looked at the golden haired child in the cradle, understanding what the doctor was saying. "You're going to use the antidote pill to save Selena." I was devoid of emotion as I spoke. "Not Noah."

"The decision isn't mine to make." He pulled a pink tablet out of the pocket of his khaki pants and held it up so I could see it. The antidote pill. "It's yours."

"Why?" I asked.

"I'm too biased to use the pill to save Selena," he said. "Saving her is the logical choice. You, on the other hand, are in love with Noah. Which makes you better equipped to make this decision than I am."

"What about Selena's parents?" I looked around, as if her parents might appear at any moment.

"Her mother died while giving birth to her," he said. "And her father isn't of this world. He won't be a part of her life until she's come of age. So what's your decision, Raven Danvers? Will you save the man you love? Or will you save the child who's destined to save the world?"

I looked at both Noah and Selena, the gravity of this decision weighing heavily on my chest. I knew what my instinct was telling me to do. But I had to make sure of it.

"What will happen if Selena dies?" I asked, focusing on the doctor again.

"The future is never set in stone," he said. "But it's likely to be a much darker future without Selena in it. Many will die. It won't be a world that any of us will want to live in."

Likely. Not *definitely*.

If I saved Noah, it wasn't definite that the future would be as bleak as the doctor claimed. Noah and I would do everything we could to fight against evil. The future would still have a chance to be a good one without Selena in it.

But not a *likely* chance.

I let out a frustrated breath. The noble choice was to save Selena. To put my selfish desires aside and do what was best for the world.

But what about what was best for me? Because a future without Noah wasn't a future I wanted to live in.

And the doctor had said it himself—the future wasn't set in stone. There had to be something we could do to stop this bleak future from happening. Prophecies were important, but we still had free will. Choosing Noah didn't mean I was cursing the world to darkness.

But choosing Noah meant I was ending the life of a child.

Could I live with that decision?

No. It would haunt me forever.

The truth was, I couldn't live with *either* decision. But a future without Noah... being ripped away from him so soon... that wasn't a life I could live with. It wasn't even a life I wanted to imagine. It hurt too much.

Losing him now would break me.

"Save Noah." The words were out of my mouth before I could analyze the decision further.

"Are you sure?" the doctor asked.

"Yes. I'm sure."

He nodded, and the entire room—Noah and Selena included—dissolved in front of me. Everything dissolved except for the doctor and me.

No, the room wasn't dissolving. It was *transforming*.

Seconds later, we were in a dark, medieval style room. There were stone walls, stone floors, and stained glass windows. I was standing in the center of the room, staring up at the doctor.

Except he was no longer dressed in the khaki pants and button down top he wore before.

He was in robes and a crown.

And he was sitting upon a majestic throne.

RAVEN

"**R**aven Danvers," he said my name in a familiar voice—the voice that had spoken to me in the cavern. "It's a pleasure to finally meet your acquaintance. I'm Arthur."

I blinked a few times, halfway expecting everything to dissolve around me again. But the room stayed the same. Down to the wooden round table in the center of it and the man sitting on the throne in front of me.

"Arthur," I repeated the name. "As in *King* Arthur?"

"One and the same." He raised his arms, motioning around himself. "Welcome to my throne room."

"I don't understand." I shook my head, still trying to make sense of it all. "What happened to Noah? And Selena?"

"They're both fine," he said as if it was no big deal.

"They were never here at all. They weren't cursed in the first place. Noah is still in his rowboat on his way to Avalon, and Selena hasn't even been born yet. That situation was just a test to see whose life you'd choose to save. To see where your true loyalty stands."

"Seriously?" I glared up at him and reached for my sword, but it was gone. Dissolved along with everything else. "One of the hardest decisions I've had to make in my life, and it wasn't even real? It was just a test?"

He might be a king, but I couldn't help it—I was angry. Who wouldn't be, after what he'd just put me through?

"Everything since you woke up in the cavern has been a test," he said. "Your soul is here in my realm, but your body is still on that rowboat headed to Avalon."

"So this is all happening in my mind," I realized. "It isn't real."

"Just because it's happening in your mind doesn't mean it isn't real," King Arthur said. "Think of it like a simulation. Every decision you made on your journey from the cave to this room with me was evaluated to see if you're worthy of entering Avalon."

"I failed. Didn't I?" I asked. "That's why the test ended after I saved Noah instead of Selena. I made the wrong decision."

"Neither decision was wrong," he said kindly.

"By saving Noah, I let Selena die. I most likely doomed the world to darkness. How's that not wrong?"

"By saving Noah, you look a leap of faith," he countered. "A bond like the one you have with Noah is rare. By choosing him, you showed you'd do anything for love. That's not a bad thing."

"But I still failed the test," I said. "That's why it ended so suddenly. Right?"

"On the contrary," he said with a knowing smile. "Your performance in the simulation was one of the best I've ever seen."

My mouth dropped wide open. "You can't be serious," I said once I got ahold of myself. "I mean, I didn't even need to fight anything. I barely did *anything*."

"You made choices that led to peace," he said. "That's far more valuable than fighting. Don't you agree?"

"I guess." I shrugged. "But I still don't feel like I did anything spectacular."

"Let me walk you through the aspects of the test." He looked around and chuckled, as if amusing himself. "Assuming you don't have anywhere else to be?"

"Sure." I reached for one of the chairs around the table, figuring we'd be here for a while. Then I realized it might not be acceptable to sit without the King Arthur's permission... especially since it looked like I was inviting myself to sit at the legendary Round Table itself. "Is it okay if I sit?" I asked.

"Make yourself comfortable."

The chair was one of those big wooden medieval plush types. I turned it around to face King Arthur's throne and took a seat.

"Let's start from the beginning," he said once I was situated. "Choosing a weapon. Three of the weapons were created with light magic, and one was created with dark, evil magic. So only one weapon in the group of four was the 'wrong' choice."

"The trident," I said instantly.

"Yes." He nodded. "It was the most powerful of the four. But a person who naturally leans to the side of good would be repulsed by it."

"I could *feel* the darkness in it when I used it," I told him. "It made me feel icky down to my core." I shuddered again just thinking about it.

"You threw it down in the middle of the field because you didn't want to touch it anymore." He chuckled. "Your soul doesn't resonate well with dark magic. Which is, obviously, a good thing. And it's what caused the 'icky' feeling you had while holding the trident."

He paused for a moment, snapped his fingers, and a glass of red wine appeared on the arm of his chair. He raised it and took a sip. "Do you want a drink?" he asked. "I can whip up anything you want."

"Hot chocolate?" It had always been a favorite of mine. Especially after a rough day.

He snapped his fingers again, and a mug of hot chocolate appeared on the table next to me.

I took a sip of it, cautious in case it was too hot. But it was the perfect temperature. And it was delicious.

"This is the best hot chocolate *ever*," I said.

"One of the perks of this realm." He smiled. "Anyway, as for the other three weapon options, they simply show what type of fighter you are," he continued. "Offensive, defensive, or distance. Your choice of the sword showed a preference to the offensive. You like to be in full control of the situation around you. Sound about right?"

"It does." I nodded. I was one of the first to admit that I could be a bit of a control freak.

Nothing wrong with that. It was better than being a flake.

"Next, you followed the path through the woods, walking through blisters and thirst," he said. "Many get frustrated and angry at this point. They don't know anything about where they're heading, and that path can seem endless. But not you. You plowed through with sheer determination."

"I thought Avalon would be at the end of the path," I

said. "I need to get to Avalon to save my mom. And to be reunited with Noah and the others."

"So your love for those close to you kept you going." He paused, as if sizing me up, and continued. "After stopping for a well deserved drink of water, you had to choose between the unicorn and the wyvern."

"Dragon," I corrected him.

He raised an eyebrow, surprised I'd interrupted.

I was surprised myself. "Sorry." I hung my head, embarrassed for interrupting a king. But I wasn't going to pretend like I was stupid, either. "But I definitely had to choose between a unicorn and a *dragon*."

"Dragons and wyverns can easily be mistaken for each other when one doesn't know how to distinguish between the two," he said. "For simplicity sake, dragons have four legs and wyverns have two. A wyvern's arms are fused to its wings, whereas a dragon's wings are a force of their own. But most importantly, dragons are shapeshifters. Wyverns are not."

"You mean there are people who can shift into a dragon, just like Noah can shift into a wolf?" I asked, shocked.

"There are," he said. "Although dragons are a unique species of shifter, thanks to their connection with the elements. And they retreated to their own realm many millennia ago. They haven't been seen on Earth since."

"Oh." I deflated, disappointed.

"You wanted to meet a dragon?" he asked.

"It would be cool," I said. "But more importantly, it sounds like dragons would be helpful in fighting against the demons. If the dragons are on our side, of course."

"They most certainly *would* be helpful," he agreed. "But only fate will tell when they return. Anyway, we're getting off course from my explanation of your performance in the simulation. Where were we?"

"My choice between the unicorn and the wyvern," I said.

"Yes, yes." He smiled and sipped his wine. "Typically, a person will make their choice. The animal they didn't choose will be insulted about not being picked, and will attack."

"Even the unicorn?" I couldn't picture Annar being so vicious.

"You should see what they can do with those horns," he said. "Anyway, when the creature not chosen attacks, it's up to the person being tested to defend themselves and survive. You, however, made your choice with grace. You treated both creatures with the respect they deserved. You gained rapport with both of them and the wyvern flew off peacefully. Needless to say, you aced that portion of the test."

"I love animals," I explained. "And I didn't want to get on the wyvern's bad side."

"You succeeded." Pride shined in his eyes as he looked down at me. "Then you continued onto my personal favorite part of the simulation. The encounter with Grendel."

"The giant?" I asked.

"Yes." He nodded. "He's unfortunately vilified in the stories told on Earth, and he *can* be scary if need be. But his soul is inherently gentle. As you saw today."

"When I freed him."

"By freeing him, you demonstrated a keen sense of observation and empathy," he said. "It earned you and your unicorn golden apples."

"Without the apples, we would have been attacked in that forest," I said.

"Many times," he confirmed. "Those who kill Grendel pay for it in the forest. They have to face off against many dangerous creatures. Only strong fighters make it through."

"So I got a free pass."

"Not at all," he said. "By showing Grendel compassion, the creatures of the forest showed you compassion in return. It was earned, and well deserved."

"Thank you." I blushed and sipped my hot chocolate.

Inwardly, I was glad I didn't have to fight the creatures of the forest. My fighting skills weren't there.

Yet.

"After the forest, your choices showed more about your character," he continued. "You chose the palace next to the sea, showing you have an affinity for water. Choosing the knowledge vial showed your wisdom, or potential for it. And then, your final choice to save Noah demonstrated your willingness to do anything for those you love. Congratulations, Raven—you're continuing onto Avalon. Your determination, empathy, and unwavering love for those close to you will be a blessing to us all."

"What about the others?" I asked. "Are they continuing onto Avalon, too?"

"You'll find out when your boat arrives to the island," he said. "But for now, I must wish you goodbye. And good luck. You have many trials ahead, but after your excellent showing in the simulation, I have no doubt you'll succeed."

I opened my mouth to ask him about the upcoming trials, but the room dissolved around me before I had a chance.

When I opened my eyes, I was back in my rowboat. And all I could see was white fog surrounding me.

RAVEN

I sat up in the boat as the fog started to clear. I could barely make out a large, mountainous island ahead, still mostly hidden in the mist.

Avalon.

Now that the fog wasn't as thick, I looked around to see who else had made it. Noah was in his boat a few feet away, looking similarly dazed.

Any anxiety I had about Noah not also making it through the simulation disappeared immediately. Of *course* he made it through. Deep in my heart, I knew he would. It just felt better seeing him and knowing for sure.

Thomas, Bella, and Jessica were there as well. But it was only the five of us.

I turned around to see if Harry, Kara, and Keith's rowboats were behind us.

They weren't. The three other humans hadn't made it through.

"Well." Bella sat straight and shook her hands off, as if she'd just come out of a battle. "That was exhilarating. Which weapon did you all choose?"

"The sword," Noah and I said in unison.

We both smiled at each other, and love shined in his eyes. I wished I could reach out to him. But our rowboats were all floating out of arm's reach of one another.

"I also chose the sword," Thomas said.

I wasn't surprised—I'd heard about the way Thomas and Noah had fought Abaddon's Locust in the field outside the bunker. Apparently he was well skilled with a sword.

"The bow and arrows." Jessica's voice was small, like she was still taking everything in.

I couldn't blame her. Now that we were back in the rowboats, everything I'd experienced in the simulation didn't quite feel real. I knew it had happened, and it was clearer than a dream. But it wasn't quite as clear as something experienced in real life.

"I chose the whip." Bella smiled and flexed her hand, as if remembering using the weapon. "It did an excellent job of taking down the creatures in the forest."

"As did the sword," Thomas said, turning to Jessica and me. "The creatures in the forest were tough to beat. Especially the tiger at the end. I'm glad the two of you made it, given your lack of experience with combat."

"I didn't have to fight the creatures in the forest," I said simply.

"What?" Bella's eyebrows knit in confusion. "Why not?"

I quickly told them about freeing Grendel and being given the golden apples. Jessica and Noah chimed in as well—they'd both freed Grendel, too. The only difference between my version and Noah's was that his animal companion was the wyvern instead of the unicorn.

"So the three of you got a free pass." Bella crossed her arms, not looking happy.

"Not a free pass," I said, recalling what King Arthur had told me. "By showing Grendel compassion, the creatures of the forest showed us compassion in return."

"And I still had to fight the wyvern." Jessica sat straighter. "An arrow in the back of its neck did the trick." She turned to me, her eyes wide in excitement. "I guess you figured out its weak spot, too. Right?"

"I didn't have to fight the wyvern, either." I shrugged

and explained what King Arthur had told me about how I'd handled the choice with grace and didn't incite the wyvern to attack.

Noah chimed in that he also didn't have to fight the animal he didn't choose.

"Seriously?" Bella looked at him in annoyance. "You're one of the best fighters in this group, and you didn't have to fight to prove yourself? At all?"

"I've got good instincts." He smirked. "And the unicorn was prideful and stubborn. I've gotten a handle on dealing with people like that these past few weeks." He looked to me and winked.

I couldn't help but chuckle, since I'd recognized the similarities between Annar and me, too.

"It makes sense that you understand animals," Thomas chimed in. "Since you're partly one yourself."

Noah brought his hands to his heart, feigning that he'd been hurt. "Better than being part machine," he said, grinning at Thomas good-naturedly.

Thomas smirked back in the way guys do when they bond over trading insults.

Bella rolled her eyes and turned to focus ahead. The moment she did, her expression switched from annoyance to wonder. "Well, would you look at that," she said, amazed.

I also turned to look ahead. The moment I did, I was sure my face had the same look of awe on it as Bella's.

Because the fog had fully cleared now, giving us an incredible view of Avalon. And wow, was it beautiful. Shaped in a giant horseshoe, the island was mountainous and bursting with life. I'd never seen a place so green. And the water around the island was bluer than the Caribbean Sea.

I took in a deep breath of fresh sea air, feeling remarkably at peace for the first time in weeks.

I felt like I was coming home.

*A*s our rowboats floated toward Avalon, we continued discussing our experiences in the simulation. There was only one part about the simulation that we avoided talking about for now. The choice between saving a loved one or saving the baby.

Some decisions were simply too personal to discuss so openly. And surely the choice hadn't been easier for any of them than it had been for me.

"Hey, Jess," Thomas interrupted Bella while she was bragging about the different ways she'd slaughtered the creatures in the forest. "How are you doing in the sun?"

Jessica touched her hands to her cheeks and gazed up at the bright sky. "I'm fine," she said, turning to Thomas. "But the sun's supposed to burn us. Right?"

Her confusion made sense. She hadn't been a

vampire for long enough to have been exposed to direct sunlight, so she didn't know what it felt like on her new skin.

"It's supposed to." He looked up at the sun in awe. "But ever since we came through the fog, it hasn't hurt at all."

"It must have something to do with Avalon," Noah mused.

"It must," Thomas agreed.

The next thing I knew, Thomas took off his white Haven top and was showing off his sculpted, muscular chest to all of us. He was just as ripped as Noah, but shades paler. I supposed that's what happens when someone hasn't gone out in the sun for decades. He leaned back to soak in the light, pure serenity on his face as he basked in the sun's warm rays.

I wished Sage were here to see this.

She *would* be here. Soon. Once we told the Earth Angel about Azazel and she sent a Nephilim to kill him, the blood bond would be broken and Sage could join us on Avalon.

"I wonder what happened to Harry and the twins," Jessica said, worry crossing her eyes. "I hope they're okay."

"They weren't accepted onto Avalon," I stated the obvious. "Jacen said a soldier from the Vale will meet them where their rowboats drop them off and bring them back to the palace. They'll be well taken care of."

Jessica nodded, satisfied with this answer.

"I doubt Avalon is a place for kids, anyway," Bella said exactly what I'd thought earlier. "They're better off returning to the Haven. Mary and the witches will take care of them until they're old enough to be turned."

"They might not want to be turned," Jessica said.

"Why wouldn't they want to be turned?" Bella looked at Jessica like she'd gone crazy. "They're humans being offered to be turned into powerful, immortal supernaturals. They'd be stupid not to accept."

Jessica shrugged, clearly not in the mood to try explaining. I understood her reluctance. Because Bella had been born as a supernatural. She didn't know anything different. I doubted she'd understand why someone might want a normal, happy human life.

Our rowboats entered the cove, and we stopped chatting to gaze around the beautiful mountainous surroundings. The island was huge—much bigger than I'd expected. The people of Avalon had enough room to spread out and make it a kingdom in itself.

Now that we were closer, I could make out a stone castle on top of one of the mountains. It was a sprawling, medieval style castle, but shiny and new. Like something out of a fantasyland.

That must be where Jacen and the Earth Angel lived.

The rowboats lined up in a single file line and turned into an inlet. They kept turning into smaller and smaller inlets until we entered a canal that took us deeper into the island. There were groups of hydrangea flowers everywhere—bursts of purples, blues, and pinks amongst all the green. It truly was a tropical paradise.

Finally, I spotted a group of people. They were working in an orchard of trees, picking a strange white fruit from the branches. As we passed, they paused from their work to smile and wave at us.

It felt like a Disney ride instead of real life. But I waved back, since it was the polite thing to do. The others in the boats did the same.

"They're a mix of shifters, witches, and vampires," Noah said from his rowboat just ahead of mine. "No Nephilim or humans."

Of course, he could smell them from here.

"The Nephilim and humans must be busy training," I said.

"Probably," he said, although the worry didn't disappear from his eyes.

Gazing back around at the people working in the orchards, I smiled wider when I spotted a familiar face —Leia, the alpha of the rougarou pack. She was surrounded by other shifters I'd met in their bar in New

Orleans. Noah had told them about Avalon when we were there. I was glad they'd decided to come to the island.

Eventually, our boats entered the mouth of a cave. It was long and winding, like a tunnel. Torches hung on the inside walls, their fire lighting the way. Again, I felt like I was on a Disney ride. Probably because the boats were magically driving themselves.

We continued through the cave for long enough that it felt like we were being taken to the center of a mountain itself. Where could the boats be bringing us?

We went around turn after turn, until I finally saw Jacen up ahead.

He was waiting on a wooden dock. Two women were there too, one on each of his sides. They wore big, fancy gowns that looked like they belonged in Medieval England, their blonde hair in curly up-dos like they were going to prom.

Maybe one of them was the Earth Angel. But Noah had mentioned to me at one point that the Earth Angel had dark hair. So neither of them could be her.

All three of them gave us warm smiles as we approached.

"Congratulations for proving your worth to King Arthur in his simulation," Jacen said once our boats stopped at the dock. "And welcome to Avalon."

KARA

I came out of a foggy sleep, still lying down in the rowboat. I'd just had a crazy dream.

All I could remember was a unicorn, and having to fight a dragon. The dragon had come at me with its teeth. I'd dropped my weapon to the ground, terror pulsing through my veins as the monster's mouth closed around my neck.

My heart raced now just thinking about it.

But as I floated along the water, the memory of the nightmare faded. Soon I couldn't remember it at all.

I needed to get up. My eyes were crusty, like I'd been crying in my sleep. But with more effort than usual, I managed to crack them open.

The thick fog still surrounded me.

Where am I? I thought.

Thanks to my gift, the exact location—down to the coordinates—popped into my mind.

I was a few miles away from the palace at the Vale.

Realization hit me like a sledgehammer. I hadn't been accepted onto Avalon. The island didn't want me.

I sat up in the rowboat, unable to see anything beyond a foot or two in front of me. "Keith?" I called for my twin through the fog.

"Kara," I heard his scared voice off to my left. "Are we almost at Avalon?"

Even though he was a boy, I'd always been the stronger, more confident twin. The one who protected him. So despite the fact that we weren't heading to Avalon, I was glad he was here with me now and that we hadn't been separated.

He'd been so excited about the idea of going to Avalon. We both had. The witches at the Haven had told us we couldn't go back home. But there was an *angel* at Avalon.

Surely an angel would reunite us with our parents. That was why we'd chosen to go to Avalon instead of staying at the Haven.

The others who had been in the bunker with us warned us not to leave. They said we were safe at the Haven. They said the angel at Avalon wanted to turn us into soldiers to fight the demons.

My brother and I didn't believe them. Our parents had told us so many stories about angels, and we'd learned about angels in Sunday school. Angels existed to protect us. To keep us safe.

If our parents had been with us, they would have told us to go to the angel. Because an angel would help us.

I'd been so sure of it. Keith and I both had been.

But we were being dumped back off at the Vale. The angel at Avalon didn't want us.

And now I had to break this terrible news to my brother.

"Kara?" Another voice echoed from my right—Harry. At least there was an adult here with us. "Can you sense where we are?"

"We're not at Avalon," I said. "We're heading back to the Vale."

"I don't want to go back there." Keith's voice trembled as he spoke. "I want to go home."

"Me too." I wrapped my arms around myself, powerless to help him.

"So do I," Harry said. "But they're only sending one supernatural to bring us back to the palace. Right?"

"That's what Jacen said," I replied. "They're sending a supernatural guard to get us so he can show us the way."

Not that I needed anyone to show me the way. With

my gift, I could easily get us back to the palace at the Vale.

But they hadn't known which of us would end up on Avalon and which of us would end up here. So obviously they had to send someone.

The fog started to clear up ahead. I could barely make out the ending of the river, and what looked like a single person waiting for us. There were lots of trees behind him—we were landing in the middle of a forest. I was now able to see my brother and Harry in their boats, too.

"I'm going to need the two of you to stay back," Harry said. "Can you do that?"

"Why?" I asked.

"Just trust me." His eyes glinted with determination as he reached for something in his pocket. "I want to go home as much as you do."

I nodded. My brother did the same.

Harry was the adult here, and this was the freest we'd been since being kidnapped by the demons. I trusted him to have a plan.

I also knew we couldn't say anything more. The supernaturals had strong senses of hearing. Whatever Harry was planning, we couldn't risk the supernatural waiting for us overhearing.

The boats moved forward out of the fog, until we

could finally see clearly. The supernatural standing at the bank of the river was a short, blond guy. He gave us a small wave and a warm smile. He looked nice.

I tensed and glanced at Harry. But he stared straight ahead at the blond supernatural, looking as determined as ever.

The blond supernatural continued smiling at us as our boats reached the shore. "Welcome back to the Vale," he said, pulling at the fronts of the boats to drag them out of the water. "I'm Will, and I've been sent here to show you the way back to the palace. I know you're probably disappointed not to have landed on Avalon. But remember—there's a grand plan going on here. You might not be meant for Avalon, but there's still a home for you at the Vale, or at the Haven—"

He didn't have time to finish his sentence.

Because Harry pulled a knife out of his pocket and threw it into his heart before he had a chance.

Will's eyes went blank, and he toppled to the ground. Dead.

I looked back and forth from Harry to Will's body in shock. "What..." I started, unsure what I even wanted to say. "Why did you do that?"

"You both want to get out of here, right?" Harry walked over to Will's body, pulled the knife out of his chest, and put it back into his pocket. I recognized the unique, swirling designs on the handle.

The knife was from the Haven. We'd all used them at the meals we'd had there.

Harry must have pocketed it when no one was looking. His gift was perfect aim. So I guessed stealing a knife made sense.

"Yeah," I said, still staring at Will's body in shock. "But you just *killed* him."

"I did what I had to do." Harry was being so harsh and cold. It scared me. But at the same time, I understood why he'd done it. He'd given us a window to escape. "Eventually, the others at the palace will notice something's wrong and will send someone out to look for him," he continued. "We need to be long gone before that happens. Can you use your sense of direction to get us to the closest town?"

I tapped into the map in my head. "There's a town about ten miles south of here," I said. "It's small, though. Really small."

"Doesn't matter," Harry said. "All I need is a phone. Then I can make a few calls and get us home." He paused and sized us up. "You kids won't have a problem walking ten miles, right?"

"We did conditioning at the bunker just like you did," Keith said. "We can handle it."

"Good." Harry nodded. "I'll cover our tracks. Probably won't matter much, since these supernaturals have insane senses of smell, but it'll help. Once we get to town we'll take a few cab rides to random locations. That should throw them off enough so they can't track us anymore. Now," he said, focusing on me again. "Every second we spend here is one more second they have to capture us and take us back to that place. I could take down one of them, but I can't take down a group of them. Are you ready to lead the way?"

"Yes." I straightened, a path forming in my mind that would get us to the town in the best time. "Let's go."

And so the three of us ran off into the forest, leaving Will, the Vale, the Haven, the bunker, and every other awful thing that had happened to us since being taken by the demons in the past.

Which was exactly where it belonged.

SKYLAR

(RAVEN'S MOM)

I sat on the bed in the same room I'd been in for the past week, flipping through the television channels mindlessly. Despite all my efforts to stop thinking about what those demons had done to me, it was all I *could* think about.

I was a monster. And it was their fault.

When they'd brought me to the attic in the house above the bunker and the vampire had sunk his fangs into my neck, I'd thought it was over. I'd prayed that wherever Raven was, she'd be safe. I'd expected that the next time I saw her would be on the other side.

Then I'd woken up. And the same demon that had taken me from my home was standing over me, smiling.

Azazel.

At the thought of his name, the scene played in my

mind again. The awful scene I'd never forget for as long as I lived.

The moment when my life had changed forever.

Even though Azazel was right in front of me, I could barely focus on him. All I could focus on was the hunger. The deep, gnawing hunger that went all the way down to my bones. It was so strong—I was consumed by it.

"She's awake," Azazel called through the doors. His eyes were red now. They definitely weren't red when he'd abducted me from my apartment. They'd been brown. "Bring him in."

The door swung open, and the vampire who'd fed from me —Dmitri, I think his name was—dragged a middle-aged man through the doors. The man was skinny and dressed in rags, like he'd been yanked from the streets.

The moment I took a breath, the scent of his blood filled my nose. The sweet smell of it made me salivate like crazy. And suddenly, I knew how to stop the hunger.

I ran to him and sank my fangs into his neck before I realized what I was doing. My body acted on impulse. Like I was an animal instead of a human.

I only realized I'd drained him dry when I was staring at his lifeless corpse on the floor and licking the last of his blood off my lips.

I backed away in horror and looked for a way to escape. But demons stood around me, blocking every exit.

I was trapped.

"What did you do to me?" I asked, even though deep down, I knew what they'd done.

The evidence was staring me straight in the face. It filled me with despair from my stomach all the way down to my toes.

"I had you turned into a vampire." Azazel smiled, confirming what I already knew was true. When he smiled, his teeth were pointed and yellow. They weren't the normal, white teeth he'd had before.

As a human, I couldn't see his true form. Now as a vampire, I could. Not just in him, but in all the other demons in the room, too. Red eyes and yellow pointed teeth.

It was a blessing humans couldn't see what demons truly looked like. They'd be terrified if they could.

"And you're not just any vampire," he continued. "You're a gifted vampire. You had a gift as a human, and that gift will be amplified since you've been turned. Now it's time to see how useful you are." He looked to a dark haired woman standing by his side. She smelled different from the others—like sickly sweet syrup. And her eyes weren't red. She wasn't a demon. "Lavinia," he said. "The complacent potion."

She removed a needle full of dark blue liquid from her weapons belt and strode toward me.

Whatever was in that syringe, I didn't want it in my body.

Azazel was standing between me and the door, but I didn't care. I made a bolt for it.

I almost made it. But two demons grabbed my arms, stopping me. I knew they were demons because of their smoky scent. Azazel had a similar scent, but stronger.

They pulled so hard it felt like my arms were about to rip out of their sockets. I cried out in pain. I would have fallen to my knees if the demons weren't propping me up and forcing me to remain standing.

Lavinia continued toward me, her predatory gaze locked on mine. "Don't worry, dear," she said with a smile. "This won't hurt a bit."

She jabbed the needle into my arm and sent the blue liquid into my veins. She was right—it didn't hurt. I felt woozy now. Relaxed. The despair, anxiety, and anger from being turned into a vampire was gone.

She'd drugged me.

Lavinia stepped to the side, and Azazel moved to stand before me. He looked smugger than ever. Like he'd won.

"Skylar," he said in a singsong-like voice. "You're going to do everything I say and answer everything I ask you honestly. Say yes to tell me you understand."

"Yes." The word came out of my lips instantly. I couldn't even think to stop it. My body was acting without my permission.

"Fantastic," he said. "You're not going to try to run again. You're only to go where I tell you to, when I tell you to." He grinned and glanced at the demon guards still holding onto me. "You can let her go. She's under my control now."

The guards did as instructed, although they remained close by. They were waiting, in case I made another attempt to escape.

I tried to run again. But I couldn't. It was like my feet were glued to the floor. I literally wasn't in control of my own body anymore.

"What did you give me?" I stared at Azazel in terror.

"Complacent potion," he said. "Brewed by my lovely witch Lavinia Foster." He gestured to the dark haired woman who'd injected me with the potion.

That must be why she smells different, I realized. She's a witch.

"As long as the potion remains in your system, you're bound to do as I ask," he continued, eyeing me up gleefully. "I know what you must be thinking now. What happens when the potion is out of my system?"

I stared at him straight on. Because yes, I was wondering how long the potion would stay in my system.

Once it was out, I'd make another run for it.

I wasn't human anymore. I was a vampire. Which meant I had a chance against the demons. A small chance, but a chance nonetheless.

"You'll be happy to know that you don't have to worry about the potion leaving your system," he said happily, as if he truly were soothing one of my worries. "If I decide to keep you, Lavinia has brewed enough complacent potion so you'll never be without it."

His eyes gleamed, and he watched me expectantly. He was getting a kick out of seeing me squirm.

So I stood straight and confident. I refused to be entertainment for a demon.

"And if you don't decide to keep me?" I asked.

"You'll want me to keep you." He grinned. "If I don't..." He paused and slashed his finger across his neck. "We have a great need for gifted vampire blood. And the blood needs to be outside of your body for us to make proper use of it."

I gulped, his message loud and clear.

If he didn't keep me, he'd kill me for my blood.

"You're right." I made an executive decision—I needed to stay alive. Not because I wanted to be a vampire. I'd honestly rather be dead than be the creature I was now. At least there'd be peace on the other side.

I needed to stay alive so I could make sure Raven never ended up in the hands of this monster. My daughter was gifted, just like me and the others in that bunker. I'd known since she was young.

I needed to keep her out of the hands of the demons. I

didn't know how I was going to do that yet. But I definitely couldn't do it if I were dead.

"I'm right about what?" He raised an eyebrow, curious.

"That I want you to keep me." The words felt vile as I spoke them, like metal in the back of my throat. But I forced myself to sound determined and resolved. A willing servant.

"Wonderful." He brought his hands together and smiled again. "I'm glad we're on the same page." He turned to look around at the others in the room. Each of them straightened when his eyes met theirs. "It's so much easier when they want to work with us," he said. "Don't you think?"

They all nodded in affirmation, gazing at him with awestruck eyes.

Puppets. All of them.

I wanted to spit at their feet. But of course, I controlled myself. For Raven's sake.

"What do you need me to do?" I asked, bringing his attention back to me.

"You're smart. I like it." He chuckled, his amusement sounding real. He was so twisted and disgusting. "Because of course you need to do something. I wouldn't keep you without you proving your worth, would I?"

I stood as still as a soldier, my hands pressed firmly to each side, waiting for his command.

Not like I had any choice to obey or not. The complacent potion had taken care of that.

His eyes turned serious, and he stepped closer so there was only a foot of space between us. "Tell me what your gift is," he said.

"I'm gifted with tarot cards." I held his gaze, refusing to let him see how terrified I truly was. "My readings are always accurate. I can interpret the cards and gain an understanding of a person's past, present, and future."

"A prophetess." He smirked, looking intrigued. "Lavinia, go fetch us a deck of tarot cards. It's time to see Skylar's gift in action."

Lavinia nodded and vanished into thin air.

"Wait," I cried out, although she clearly couldn't hear me, since she was gone. So I turned to Azazel and continued, "I do my best readings with my own deck." I sounded so meek—so unlike myself. I hated it. "It's called Crystal Visions. It's in my apartment. In the kitchen."

Where I did my last reading with Raven.

"You'll do a reading with whatever deck Lavinia brings here." He snarled. "And you better make sure it's a good one. Your life depends on it."

He glared down at me until I submitted.

"I'll do my best," I said.

"Wrong answer."

I pressed my lips together and tried again. "Okay." I made sure to sound confident this time. "I'll do it."

"Wrong again." He paced and shook his head, like he was

245

scolding a puppy that was misbehaving. "The correct answer is, 'Yes, Your Grace.'" He stopped walking and stared down at me in challenge. "Say it."

I clenched my fists, wishing I could punch him in the face. I would have done it, if the complacent potion would let me. And if I didn't think it would get me killed.

Right now, my only focus was on not getting killed. There wasn't one person in this room who would hesitate to kill me or who didn't want me dead. And they all answered to Azazel.

So I needed to make sure Azazel didn't want me dead. Which meant I needed to prove myself useful. No matter how disgusting I felt while doing so.

"Yes, Your Grace," I forced out, pushing down nausea as I submitted again to this vile monster.

"There you go." He nodded, looking pleased with himself. "That wasn't so hard, was it?"

I shook my head, hating myself more and more with each passing second.

Luckily, Lavinia soon returned with a tarot deck. The Crow's Magic deck. It was one of the decks sold at Tarotology, so I was somewhat familiar with it. It was dark, modern, and geometric—the exact opposite of my Crystal Visions deck. But I could work with it.

"Crow's Magic," I said. "Interesting choice."

"We had it lying around our apothecary." Lavinia

shrugged and handed the deck to me. "Let's see what you can do."

I glanced at the bare table and chairs on the side of the room. "Do you mind if I sit, Your Grace?" I asked Azazel. "It's best to sit while reading the cards."

"Go ahead." He followed me over to the table and sat in the chair across from mine.

The demons, vampires, and witch in the room all gathered around to watch. They kept their expressions neutral. But I could tell from the way they leaned forward that they were interested in seeing what I could do.

I was interested to see what I could do, too. Because if Azazel was right, and being a vampire amplified my powers... well, I was certainly curious about what was about to happen when I read the cards.

I removed the cards from the deck and started to shuffle them. "Is there anything in particular you want to know from the cards?" I asked Azazel.

"As a matter of fact, there is." He leaned back into the small wooden chair, making himself comfortable. "As you know, I'm sending demons out to various places around the country to hunt down gifted humans and bring them to me. Unfortunately, my demons are being hunted by two wolf shifters. The shifters are wearing cloaking rings that make them impossible to track. So I'd like for you to tell me where these shifters will be next, so I can capture them before they

kill any more of my demons. Do you think you can do that?"
He gave me a chilling smile—a smile that let me know if I
couldn't do what he asked, I was as good as dead.

My heart dropped into my stomach. Because the cards
weren't that specific. They gave general ideas of the future,
but finding two wolf shifters? That wasn't what the cards were
designed to do.

"I'll do my best." My voice shook as I spoke.

"We'll see if that's enough." He smiled again, showing me
his yellowed, pointed teeth.

They apparently didn't have toothbrushes in Hell.

I continued shuffling the deck, focusing on Azazel's ques-
tion. Where were these wolf shifters who were hunting his
demons? The necessary spread for the question being asked
always came to me while I was shuffling. I supposed it was
part of my gift.

Now, my intuition was telling me to do a simple one card
draw.

Strange. For a question this specific, I expected a more
complex spread. But I knew better than to doubt my intuition.
If it wanted me to do a one card draw, then that's what I'd do.

Once finished shuffling, I fanned the cards out flat on the
table. "Pick one card and hand it to me face down," I told
Azazel.

He let his hand linger above the cards, eventually pulling one from the center of the spread. He handed it to me and I flipped it over.

The Five of Swords.

In this deck, the Five of Swords featured an angel looking out at the solar system. The words "distress" and "confusion" were written under its name. The words made sense with the card. In my Crystal Visions deck, this card showed a woman and man, both stabbed in the backs with swords.

It was the card of betrayal.

But how did it relate to the hunters killing Azazel's demons? I needed to figure out something to say to him. My life depended on it.

I stared at the card, willing the answer to come to me.

Suddenly, the image on the card changed. I was no longer looking at the geometric angel staring out at the solar system.

I saw Raven and a dark haired girl heading out from a club. There was a demon between them, their arms linked with his. They turned and led him down the street. Two attractive men in their mid-twenties came out of the club soon afterward, clearly following them.

Fury raced through my veins. I wanted to tell Raven to run as far as she could. Because I knew what was happening. The demon had targeted her as a gifted human. He was leading her away so he could bring her to that awful bunker.

"Turn around," I said. "Don't go with him."

They didn't hear me. They simply continued walking, turning down another, less crowded street.

I tried to take in as much information as possible about where they were. Street signs, the buildings they passed, everything. The license plates mostly said Illinois on them. From the looks of the city, they appeared to be in Chicago.

What was Raven doing in Chicago? I knew most of her friends, but I didn't recognize the dark haired girl with her. Perhaps the girl was another gifted human.

Unable to influence what happened in the scene before me, I kept watching carefully. It was nighttime there and daytime here. This was a future reading, which meant at minimum, this was happening tonight.

Horror built in my throat as Raven and her friend walked into an alley with the demon. What was Raven thinking? I'd taught her better than to follow strangers into alleys. This scene before me made no sense.

The demon had a horribly smug look on his face, like he knew he had them.

Suddenly, the dark haired girl pulled a knife from her boot. She struck at the demon, who quickly brought out a knife of his own to defend himself. Raven scurried to the wall, staying out of the fight.

The dark haired girl moved supernaturally fast as she traded blows with the demon. She wasn't human.

She must be one of the wolf shifters hunting down the demons.

How on Earth had Raven gotten involved with them?

The answer came to me quickly. Because it was me. Raven must have gotten involved with the shifters because of my being taken.

The dark haired girl was still holding her own against the demon as the two men in their twenties burst into the alley. The rugged, brown haired man pulled out a dagger and joined in the fight. The dark haired one in the suit stood near Raven, protecting her.

But now that it was two against one, it didn't take the brown haired man long to jab his dagger through the demon's heart. Horror passed over the demon's eyes, right before he turned into a pile of dust.

Raven watched the rugged, brown haired man fight the demon, love shining in her eyes. Once the demon was dead, she jumped up in excitement. She, the man who'd been protecting her, and the dark haired girl all celebrated the win.

The rugged, brown haired man kneeled into the pile of ash and plucked something out of it.

That was the final thing I saw before the scene disappeared and the tarot card returned to normal.

I looked back up at Azazel in shock. Because I'd always gotten a sense of the future from the cards. But to actually see the future play out in front of me? That was new.

I needed to tell him as little as possible while still giving him enough information" to deem me useful. Above everything, he couldn't know about Raven. And he definitely couldn't know she was my daughter. I hated to think about what he'd do with that information if he had it.

With the complacent potion in my system, I'd be forced to tell him what he wanted to know. But there were ways to tell some of the truth while omitting the parts I wanted to hide. It would be difficult. But I had to do my absolute best, to keep Raven safe.

If there was a way to keep Raven safe. Now that she was involved with these hunters, she was putting herself in danger. And I couldn't help her.

I sent up a silent prayer to the Goddess to protect my Raven.

"Well?" Azazel asked. "Do you know where the hunters will be next?"

"What do these hunters look like?" I answered his question with one of my own.

"One female, one male," he said. "Mid-twenties. The girl has long, almost black hair and the guy has brown hair. Both of them are fit. When I last saw them, they were wearing lots of leather."

"I saw them," I confirmed. "When I looked into the card, I saw them trap and kill your demon."

"Where were they?" he leaned forward, hungry for infor-

mation. And because of the complacent potion, I had no choice but to answer.

"Chicago."

He narrowed his eyes. "Where in Chicago? My demons hunt for gifted humans in clubs and bars. It makes it easier to find and coerce them. Did you see the name of the place they were in?"

"Yes," I said.

"What was it called?"

Thanks to the complacent potion, I rattled off the name of the club they'd come out of, like it was nothing at all.

I set the card on the table and stared down at it, horrified.

I'd just betrayed my own daughter. And because of the complacent potion, there was nothing I could do about it.

Azazel asked me more information about the hunt. I had no choice but to tell him about how the hunters had followed the demon into the alley, attacked, and killed him.

I hated myself more and more with every traitorous word that came out of my mouth.

Luckily he didn't suspect there were more than two hunters. And I didn't volunteer the information.

"Impressive." Azazel crossed his arms and looked at me with admiration. "Looks like you're going to be useful after all." He rotated around in his chair and focused on Lavinia. "The club Skylar saw in Chicago is where Alex is hunting tomorrow night. So I'm going to need you to make me a trans-formation potion with Alex's DNA."

"What are you planning?" Lavinia shot him a conniving smile.

"I'll be taking Alex's place." He stood and brushed his hands off on his leather jacket, looking ready for a fight. "Those hunters are in for a surprise. Because that future our handy little prophetess just saw? I'm going to change it."

I sat back in dread, wishing I'd been able to keep my mouth shut. Now Raven was in danger. It was my fault. And thanks to the complacent potion, there was nothing I could do about it.

"Oh, and Skylar?" Azazel looked back at me, that evil glint still in his eyes. "Congratulations. You're the first gifted vampire we're bringing onto our team. Welcome to the dark side."

"Where should we put her?" Lavinia asked.

"Leave her here for now," he said. "Keep her well guarded." He aimed that last part at the demon and vampire guards surrounding me. "Thanks to what she just told me, I'll be bringing Sage back to her pack tomorrow night. Which means the Montgomery pack will be blood binding with me soon. Once they're blood bound, their compound can be our home base. We'll come get Skylar once the ceremony is complete. Now, let's go tell Alex about our change in plan. Because I've got myself some hunters to catch."

Azazel hadn't requested a tarot reading from me since that first one in the attic.

I was just stuck here, in this room. I had a television and books to keep me occupied. The complacent potion kept me from opening the window or leaving through the door. The room was nice and plush, but it didn't matter. It might as well have been a jail cell.

Twice a day, a Foster witch came in with a serving of blood and a needle of complacent potion. I knew they were Foster witches because they had that syrup smell to them, and they looked like Lavinia. Dark hair, and skin so pale it looked like they'd never seen the sun. None of them spoke to me. They simply gave me the shot, placed the blood on the table, and left.

As someone who'd been a vegan since middle school, I *hated* drinking blood to survive. Worst of all, I hated how much my body loved it. How delicious it smelled. How much I salivated for it whenever it was brought into the room.

I'd tried not drinking it. My first day here, I'd flushed the blood down the toilet.

I'd ended up in bed all day, the hunger consuming me down to my bones. When the witch finally came back with my next drink, I'd finished it all in one delicious gulp.

Flushing it down the toilet had been too torturous to try again. Since then, I'd tried leaving the blood on the table and seeing how long I could go without it.

The longest I'd gone was nine hours. Nine awful hours of staring at the blood like an addict, needing my next fix.

Eventually, the hunger became so strong that I couldn't resist.

This was what I was now. A vampire. I needed blood to survive like a human needed food. Without it, I'd die.

But there had to be humane ways to get that blood. Ways that didn't involve killing.

Once I got out of here, I'd figure out a solution. For now, I had no choice but to drink the blood given to me. It was that or die.

And I didn't want to die. Because the demons that had done this to me… they had hell to pay.

On my seventh day in this miserable room, Lavinia herself came in to give me my meal and dose of complacent potion. But there was something else on her silver tray, too.

A tarot deck. Crystal Visions.

She placed the tray down on the table and stared at me. She looked like she had something to say.

I stared back, daring her to speak first.

"Your punishment is over," she finally said.

"Punishment?" I sat back and tilted my head, unsure what she was talking about.

"Azazel knows you didn't tell him the truth about what you saw in the tarot card," she said. "That's why he's keeping you locked in this room. He knows your daughter was with the hunters. Raven, I believe he said her name was?"

I simply continued to stare at her, saying nothing.

"No matter." She shrugged. "I'm sure you'll be thrilled to know that not only is Raven alive, but she escaped the bunker. She freed everyone in there. And now, thanks to inside information, we believe she's on her way to Avalon."

"Avalon?" I repeated, dumbfounded. "You mean the island from Arthurian legend?"

"One and the same," she said. "It's where the Earth Angel is raising her army to fight the demons. The angels have hidden the island's location from us. So Azazel has commanded you to use your gift with the tarot cards to help us find it."

Because of the push of the complacent potion, I walked over to the table where the deck of cards sat, removed them from the box, and started shuffling.

Stupid complacent potion, forcing me to follow that disgusting demon's commands.

"Oh, and Skylar?" Lavinia added. "Your punishment is only over if you tell me what I need to know. Withhold information again, and you'll remained locked in here."

"And if I tell you what you want to know, will you let me go home?" I asked.

She threw back her head and laughed. "Good heavens, no," she said. "You'll be allowed free reign of the Montgomery compound, but you won't be able to leave the premises. We're keeping you safe here. We can't let anything bad happen to our prophetess, can we now?"

"Of course not," I said automatically as I continued shuffling the cards.

As I was shuffling, she walked over and jabbed me with the needle full of complacent potion. She was clearly making extra sure I'd tell her the full truth this time.

I glared at her and kept doing what I was doing.

Eventually I stopped shuffling and spread the cards out on the table. I thought about the question—the location to Avalon—reached for a card, and plucked it from the spread.

The Three of Wands.

The imagery on this card was one of my favorites in

the deck. It was a young woman holding a glowing crystal ball, gazing out at the horizon. A dragon and a lioness relaxed near her, also admiring the view.

On a general level, the card represented exploration, new adventure, and possibilities. But like before, the image on the card shifted until I was no longer staring at the drawing.

Now it was a scene playing out before me. The scene was from the near past. I didn't know how I knew that— I just did.

Three people in rowboats—a young girl, a young boy, and a middle-aged man—floated down a foggy river and approached a shore. I instantly recognized them from my time in the bunker. The twins were Kara and Keith. The man was Harry. He'd shared my table at mealtimes.

Another man was waiting for them at the shore. But Harry removed a knife from his pocket and flung it straight into the other man's heart.

Of course he did. His gift was perfect aim.

Harry told Kara to use her sense of direction to get them out of there. She led the way, the three of them running through the densely packed forest toward the nearest town.

The scene shimmered and changed, and I somehow

knew I was no longer looking at the past. Now, I was seeing the future.

Harry, Kara, and Keith had escaped to the closest town. From there, they took a taxi to the closest city. Banff, in Alberta, Canada. They checked into a chain hotel near the airport.

The scene changed again. It was now the next morning. The twins' parents arrived to pick them up. They had a joyful reunion that brought tears to my eyes, and caused a deep longing to be reunited with my own daughter. Harry saw the four of them off on their flight, and then left for his own flight that would take him back home to his wife.

The scene faded again, leaving me staring at the true artwork on the Three of Wands card.

"Well?" Lavinia crossed her arms, watching me impatiently. "Tell me what you saw. Don't leave anything out this time."

The words came rushing out of my mouth—every single detail of what I'd seen in the card, down to the name of the hotel where Harry and the twins would stay. The complacent potion made it impossible to keep anything to myself.

I hated myself the entire time I spoke. I was a traitor. I cared about these three people, yet here I was, taking their future happiness away from them.

"How's this related to the location of Avalon?" Lavinia asked once I was done.

"The cards didn't say." I shrugged. "I asked for help locating the island, and that's what they showed me."

"Very well." She looked at me suspiciously, gathered up the cards, and took them back. She clearly didn't intend for me to have access to the deck without supervision. "I'll have Azazel send a team of demons to this hotel to capture the gifted humans. They may have gotten away in the future you saw, but we'll change it. Just like we changed the future you saw of the shifters killing Alex in Chicago."

Dread twisted in my stomach. Because I knew what Kara's gift was. As would Azazel, once he had her back in his clutches.

She had a perfect sense of direction.

If she was turned into a vampire, her gift would be heightened.

And then, she would become the perfect tool Azazel needed to locate Avalon.

Thank you for reading The Angel Island! I hope you loved this book as much as I loved writing it.

The next book in the series—The Angel Secret—is out now! The Angel Secret is the second to last book in the Angel Trials series.

Grab The Angel Secret on Amazon ➜ CLICK HERE

You can also check out the cover and description below. (You might have to turn the page to view the cover.)

Welcome to Avalon Academy—where supernaturals train, and only the strong survive.

After a long journey across the country, Raven has finally made it to the hidden island of Avalon. But she can't rest yet. Because she still needs to enter the Angel

Trials, become a Nephilim, and save her mom from the greater demon holding her hostage.

She knew the Angel Trials were going to be hard. But nothing could prepare her for what she learns when she gets to Avalon. Because the leader of the island—the Earth Angel—has been keeping a secret.

A secret so devastating it could ruin all hope of the supernaturals ever winning the war against the demons.

Get ready for more twists and turns in The Angel Secret, the sixth book in the addicting Dark World: The Angel Trials urban fantasy series!

**GRAB THE ANGEL SECRET ON AMAZON NOW →
CLICK HERE**

ABOUT THE AUTHOR

Michelle Madow is a USA Today bestselling author of fast paced fantasy novels that will leave you turning the pages wanting more! Her books are full of magic, adventure, romance, and twists you'll never see coming.

Click here or visit author.to/MichelleMadow to view a full list of Michelle's novels on Amazon.

To get free books, exclusive content, and instant updates from Michelle, visit www.michellemadow.com/subscribe and subscribe to her newsletter now!

THE ANGEL ISLAND

Published by Dreamscape Publishing

ISBN: 9781791668129

❀ Created with Vellum

Made in the USA
Middletown, DE
12 April 2019